GOSPEL OF THE CUCKOO

A DREAD SOUTH NOVELLA

BY SIRIUS

GOSPEL OF THE CUCKOO

SIRIUS

GOSPEL OF THE CUCKOO

A Dread South Novella

SIRIUS

THE LAUGHING MAN HOUSE PUBLISHING

GOSPEL OF THE CUCKOO

ISBN: 9798218417604

www.uncrownednovel.com

Cover Design by Geoff Parrell

Illustrated by Rachel Dougherty
https://x.com/Swifty_f0x

Edited by Janus

Royalty-Free images sourced by Pixabay

Praise for
Gospel of the Cuckoo

"If you like your horror queer and richly gothic, Gospel of the Cuckoo commands your attention with its unrepentant storytelling, gritty wit, authentic inclusivity, and striking prose. Get your hands on Sirius' new novella!"

-Kayli Scholz, author of "Saint Grit"

"Engrossing from page one, Gospel of the Cuckoo is as engaging as it is horrifying. A sucker punch of a novella, sexy and blasphemous with a heavy dose of darkness. I loved it."

-Sonora Taylor, award-winning author of
"Little Paranoias: Stories and Seeing Things"

"Sirius is the voice of a generation, preaching delicious sacrilege. If you like your horror hot, southern, and diverse, Gospel of The Cuckoo delivers on all fronts and puts an erotic edge on religious horror."

-Ravven White, author of "Haunted Hallways"

This one is for my Papaw.
It's not that I think you would have liked it,
it's just that I wrote it for you anyway.
I hope you've had peace in your mansion of gold
on the other side of the pearly gates.

ALSO BY SIRIUS

The Draonir Saga
Uncrowned
Partitioned
Condemned
Disinherited*

The Draonir Saga: Iconoclasts
Hawthorne: A Draonir Novella
The Red Star Society

The Gentlemen Demon Series
Swallow You Whole
Sever Your Spine

The Wire Killers Novellas
Birdeater

The Dread South Series
Rising Sun Over the Devil's Nest
Blackjack + Moonshine
Gospel of the Cuckoo
Funny Little Town
Late Night Testament

*TBA

CHAPTER ONE

HOLY GROUND

Blessing Easton was born dead and veiled. He slid out of his mother's womb in an unruptured amniotic sac and was blue in the face as if he had been holding his breath the entire time. His mother held him against her chest and sobbed, and the minute she cursed God, she heard her child let out a ragged cry. She called him 'little boy blue' every day after that, and although she was long-dead, he was still Blue to everyone who knew him best. He was Blue to the congregation, because they were his family. He loved them above all, except God. God came first. God always came first.

Dallas had heard it all before. At least once a month, the service was the same. Reverend Blue loved to tell the story of his 'death and resurrection' that made him a 'bona fide modern-day Lazarus, amen!'

The congregation loved it, too. It was only in their small town of Wicker, Alabama that you could find a reverend who had been born again twice. Everything ticked on the reverend's clock because every non-taxpaying dollar went straight into the Church of New Lazarus' collection plate. The doors were open every day of the week with deacons assigned to work in shifts in case some poor soul needed shepherding at 3AM.

Dallas rubbed his eyes and adjusted himself in the pew, hoping that sitting up straight would be enough to chase away the piling exhaustion that kept dragging down his eyelids. A stab of pain in his lower back reminded him of why he had been slouching in the first place, and he pushed an ugly hiss through his nose to try and stop himself from swearing.

The Church of New Lazarus was a single-wide trailer that had been gutted and filled with secondhand pews and mismatched hymnals that had been donated from other, bigger churches. Blue's voice thundered off the narrow walls and his pounding foot shook the pink carpet-covered platform where his pulpit was bolted down. He liked to slam his hand on the thick, weathered bible that sat on top of the pulpit and knock aside the little microphone that clipped onto the side. He was young, and handsome, but he spat out gospel like an old-timer. He used colloquialisms that had been out of style for nearly three decades but made the old ladies nod their heads and holler.

Dallas winced and pinched the foam earplug that was already wedged into his ear canal. He pushed it in a little deeper before adjusting the other side to match. Nothing could block out Blue's voice entirely, especially once he got hot, but dimming it helped. Otherwise, it was unbearable. And it was not like Dallas hated the sermon. He admired Blue just as much, if not more, than everyone else. Blue's version of God was different in a way that Dallas really liked, but God still did not pay his bills—or change his grandfather's bedding in the small hours of the morning.

The sermon started winding down to the tune of an electric keyboard that Reverend Blue continued to talk over. The pianist was the same woman who taught Dallas algebra in high school, and she was better at math than reading sheet music. It didn't make a lick of difference to the congregation, with heads popping up one-by-one and slick dress shoes shuffling towards the front of the church with blubbering prayers already on their lips.

Dallas shrank back in the pew and tried to make himself as small as possible. The altar call was the part that he hated—mostly because everyone felt the need to place their hands against his shoulders and propel him towards the center where they could circle him like vultures. If he waited long enough, they would all move past, and he could grab his cane and slink out through the door.

Marge Elsie, who always wore the biggest hats, shot him an encouraging smile as she set both hands on the back of the pew in front of her and stood up. She waved her arm, gesturing for him to come forward, and he just smiled back and nodded. He wrapped his fingers around the head of his cane and squeezed so hard that his knuckles went white. His back protested again as he slid towards the other side of the pew and crept out, desperately hoping to escape further notice. He felt Marge Elsie's eyes on him, but he did not stop to glance back.

The sun beat down mercilessly on the unsheltered churchyard, but Dallas did not dare remove his jacket, even though he was sweating. Slipping out during the altar call was one thing, but he was not ballsy enough to shed a single article of modest clothing or walk home without Reverend Blue's benison. The red jacket was loosely woven cotton and completely shapeless, concealing the fact that the matching shirt he wore tucked into his pants hugged his narrow waist a little too closely. Red and white, the blood and the light of Christ—easy colors to find with easy patterns to sew. The church only issued out two—and there was a designated group within the congregation who could whip them out fairly quickly. Dallas had made his own, which somehow made his resentment for the jacket even worse—especially since the collar kept rubbing against his sweaty neck and making him itch.

By the time church let out, his knees were starting to shake. Dallas kept one hand on the wooden banister that ran alongside the dirty concrete steps and gripped his cane with the other.

Finally the door opened, and Reverend Blue was the first to step out. The sunlight hit his wavy golden hair and transformed him into a glowing saint, while his light blue eyes shimmered like twin prisms left dangling from a front porch beam. His bespoke red suit and his gold bird-shaped bolo tie were bright and new, made of better material than anyone else had access to in the congregation. Between his tie, the gold bands on his slim fingers, and the small gold hoop dangling from his earlobe—he was probably wearing a year's worth of their salaries in jewelry alone. The face of his Rolex watch flashed whenever he flicked his busy wrists. The eye of God Himself throwing a casual wink.

"Nice to see your face as always, Dallas," the reverend spoke. He had a voice like honey whiskey—a little too sweet to be pleasant. Dallas averted his eyes, fixing them on the mirror-like surfaces of Blue's shiny church shoes.

"Fearsome sermon today, reverend," Dallas muttered. "I took notes for my grandfather. He wanted me to tell you that he is sorry to have missed it."

"If there is anyone who has a reason to miss service, it is your grandpa." Reverend Blue raised his hand and Dallas flinched. The reverend brought his fingertips down to rest against the young man's shoulder, and Dallas felt cold all the way down to his insides—his heart was suddenly made of lead and had forgotten how to beat.

The congregation was staring at him. He could feel every single burning eye boring into the sides of his head. All the heat was escaping through Dallas' face and he knew that his cheeks were red, but he still did not raise his head. He would not have, for anything.

"Dallas Hackett," Reverend Blue spoke in that booming, authoritative tone. "Take this benison to your grandfather. I want him running to church tomorrow evening, nothing excused. God will have it so."

"God will have it so," the congregation echoed behind him.

Dallas swallowed hard and pulled his cane closer to his side. He nodded and finally found the guts to raise his eyes, although it was not quite enough to meet the reverend's gaze.

"Do we believe the Lord can do it?" Reverend Blue asked. He still had not pulled his fingers back, and Dallas' shoulder was starting to feel numb.

"Blessed! Blessed!" the congregation chanted. Dallas pulled in another shaky breath through his nose and fought to suppress the fear that clawed at his stomach like a trapped animal.

"What about you, Dallas?" The reverend grabbed his chin and forced it up so that his soft, ice-blue eyes—so pale they barely held any color at all—could arrest Dallas' golden-green ones. "Do you believe in the Lord?"

"With all my heart," Dallas' throat convulsed as he swallowed, "reverend."

Reverend Blue smiled. All of a sudden, Dallas felt warm again. The heat raced through his veins and made his whole lower half clench, as if he suddenly had to use the bathroom. When the reverend released his chin, Dallas fell back. He tried to catch his balance on his cane, but it was not stable enough to support him. He dropped to his knees on the ground, wincing as he hit the dirt. His dark jeans caught the worst of it in long, dragging stains down the front of his knees.

The reverend turned his attention elsewhere, and so did the rest of the congregation behind him. Everyone continued to clamor for his touch, grasping at his hands or tugging on his suit jacket while exclaiming over the sermon and muttering frantically over their own need for a blessing. Dallas ground his teeth and dug his cane into the dirt, using it as leverage to pull himself back up to his feet.

He swayed a little once he was upright, but regained his balance fairly quickly.

He took a few steps before pausing again. Dallas made sure that no one was looking as he peeled away his jacket, tying the arms around his waist before continuing on his way.

CHAPTER TWO

PASS ME NOT

The austere white house with two proud stories and a balcony that wrapped around its top level was once the nicest home in Wicker. Its rapid decline into disrepair had come about in the last five years, when Dallas' grandfather fell ill with a crippling fever he never quite recovered from—which was around the same time the Church of New Lazarus opened its doors.

The wooden steps that led up to the front door were too dangerous to climb, with the flat heads of rusted nails sticking up from their rotted centers. The stairs going up to the back door were not much better. The mortar had crumbled and come loose between the bricks to the point where one misstep was likely to separate them from each other and send the person tumbling. Dallas avoided the most problematic ones by taking the steps two at a time. The dingy porch door with its torn screen groaned as he pulled it open to make his way inside.

Even though it was the middle of August, the house was freezing. Dallas kicked off his shoes quickly and rubbed his arms, trying to knock off the clammy chill that came from the sudden change in temperature. From the other side of the kitchen wall, popping vinyl skipped over the grainy crooning of reedy tenors singing old Southern Gospel hymns. It never stopped; it was the only thing that brought Andy Hackett any comfort.

Dallas stashed his shoes and crept across the linoleum on his toes. He peered into the living room, trying to get a glimpse of his grandfather without disturbing him—especially if the man was asleep. A deep snore like a revving lawnmower overtook the room. When Dallas glanced at his grandfather, the old man was still in his favorite recliner—one grizzled cheek resting against his shoulder with bunched-up folds of loose skin obscuring his neck.

The record ended and Dallas relished the long silence that trailed after it. He was in no hurry to flip it over any sooner than he had to. He pulled himself back into the kitchen to start the process of making sandwiches for their lunch, even though his legs hurt and all he wanted to do was plant himself face-down into his pillow and nap.

Spam, cubed pickles, and American cheese on white Wonder bread. All of it straight from the church pantry. The bread was a little stale and the cheese was a bit gummy—

but it all beat starving. Dallas had absolutely eaten worse things.

"Delta?" His grandfather's voice, muzzy with sleep, called out from the living room. Dallas made a face at the use of his deadname, even though his grandfather could not see his expression.

It was one of those things that he knew shouldn't matter, all things considered, yet it did.

"I'm making lunch," Dallas raised his voice. "I'll be right there."

"The music stopped."

"I'll put it back on." Dallas scooped up one of the paper plates from the counter and started towards the living room. "I went to church this morning. Everyone asked how you were doing."

He entered in time to see his grandfather struggling to sit upright, digging his hands into the puffy arms of his chair and scooting backwards with a low grunt. A patch of Andy's thick white hair stuck straight up from the back of his head like the plume of a cockatoo. Dallas rolled his lips inward to try and keep his smile from curling out of control.

"Did you take notes?" Andy grunted again as he shifted his hips and settled back into his seat. Soft, crinkling paper rustling against leather reminded Dallas that some post-lunch cleanup might be in order.

"I did." Dallas set the paper plate down on top of a wooden tray table and dragged it over to his grandfather's chair. "I told the reverend that you—"

"Did you give him the cheque?" Andy cut him off. Dallas blinked and stammered out his response as he adjusted the blanket over his grandfather's lap.

"Yes," he said. "I mean—yes, sir. I put it in the collection plate when they took tithe."

"Good, good." Andy seemed to relax a bit. He reached out for his plate and pulled it a little closer to start eating. "Was it a good service?"

"Of course. Same as always. I'll get my notes for you." Dallas straightened. "Do you want me to read them to you while you eat?"

"That would be fine." Andy peeled up the layers of his sandwich to peek between them. "And bring me a soda from the fridge."

Dallas did as he was told. He grabbed two glass bottles of cream soda as well as his own plate, balancing it on top of his yellow notepad as he took it all back to the living room. He twisted the metal cap off one of the bottles and set it down on the wooden tray table within his grandfather's reach.

"It wasn't anything groundbreaking," he said, trying to keep things lighthearted. "It was a Resurrection Sunday."

His grandfather snorted and stuck a finger into his mouth, fishing around in his back teeth for whatever was stuck between them.

"He's a good preacher," Andy said half-muffled, "but he loves to tell that story. It is important, I guess."

"The congregation likes it." Dallas finally settled into his own chair. "It reminds them of why they believe."

"The truly faithful don't bear so much reminding," Andy shot back. "I was a believer from the beginning, and I have never let my faith waiver—not once. Do you remember that? Do you remember the reverend telling me that I was truly faithful, and that the church would stand to have more men like me?"

Dallas peeled the stiff crust off his bread and did not look up. "Yes, sir," he said. "I remember." It was impossible to forget the way Blue's shiny cornflower irises had turned almost purple when he lowered his hand to rest against Andy Hackett's shoulder. His voice had rumbled in the way of distant thunder—soft and full of foreboding in a way that made your bones ache.

Dallas had been scared of him, but Andy Hackett soaked up the words like they were water spattering against parched ground. Dallas half-expected his grandfather to fall to his knees and kiss the shoes of the reverend right then and there.

It was all so sudden and strange, how the entirety of Wicker had just been swallowed up by this one man who had been dropped into their midst as if by some mysterious divine hand.

"Delta?" His grandfather's voice yanked him back.

"Sorry," Dallas choked on a piece of his sandwich and held up his hand in front of his mouth.

"I asked if there was anything else interesting." Andy Hackett had polished off his sandwich and was slurping up his soda from the glass bottle.

Blue's parting benison scratched at the back of Dallas' skull—an unwelcome intruder, crawling like a silverfish that had gotten netted into his hair. He swallowed down a hard lump that came bobbing back up as quickly as his throat could constrict. The words formed a ball on the back of his tongue and made him choke again. He gagged until he thought he was going to give up his lunch, and a swig of fizzy soda did nothing but make it worse.

Dallas tried to swallow again and opened his mouth to speak. The soda froth came spilling down the sides of his mouth and he wiped it away with a crumpled napkin, coughing into the smeary depths. When he finally raised his head, the voice that came out of his mouth was not his own. It sounded like Reverend Blue, although the deep booming version—where the simple act of speaking was enough to make it feel like there was fire racing down his esophagus.

"I want your grandfather running to church tomorrow evening, nothing excused," Dallas quoted. "God will have it so." When he finished speaking, he realized his fingertips were digging into his thigh. He let out a gasp and dropped his head, swinging it to the side to spit the last of the froth into his napkin.

A strange look crossed his grandfather's face. Dallas had never seen the old man look so serene—or so blank. His cloudy brown eyes stared forward and his jaw slackened enough so that his lips hung open, and for a moment, Dallas' heart leapt in fear that he might be having a stroke.

Dallas was halfway out of his chair before his grandfather recovered. Andy Hackett shook his head and pushed his fingers down the corners of his mouth, ending to pinch the flap of skin right above his Adam's apple.

"Well," he said. "If that was what the reverend said, then that is what I must do."

"I don't think he meant it literally," Dallas said, his words shaking just a little. "He just wanted you to know the congregation misses you is all."

Andy waved his hand dismissively.

"If he believes, then I believe," he said. "And through God I can do anything. So make sure to have my suit pressed for tomorrow—and my tie, too. I won't look like I came crawling out of bed."

"But—" Dallas began to protest, but a hard look from his grandfather stole the rest of his argument.

Andy Hackett was Alabama-stubborn through and through. There was no getting around him, once he had made up his mind.

There was always the chance that he might have a change of heart, especially if he started feeling poorly, but Dallas couldn't count on that.

CHAPTER THREE

JOY UNSPEAKABLE

Andy Hackett started getting ready for church at three o' clock in the afternoon, and Dallas was there to assist him at every step. He started by grabbing the blue edges of the absorbent pad that was wedged between his grandfather and the chair and tugging. It helped lift his grandfather up high enough that he could clean out the piss that was left smeared over the leather, and then he pulled the pad out altogether. His grandfather had once been the biggest, burliest man he knew. The past few years had reduced him to a shriveled husk of his former self, to the point where he was gaunt and weak with a neck that was too stiff to turn and feet that were too swollen to walk much of anywhere. He didn't know just how the man planned to rise and join the joyful congregation, but he was leaving all that between Andy and God.

He felt bad enough that he had not disturbed his grandfather's nap enough to check on the diaper. Now, everything had soaked through, and the bed pants would need to be washed. Dallas dismissed that to the back of his mind for the moment and wiped his grandfather down. It was a humiliating task for them both. There were parts of a grown man that his grandchildren were never meant to see. But someone had to do it—and Andy was too weak.

The labor made Dallas' knees shake and sent shooting pains up his spine. The increasing agony played second fiddle to his guilt. He was young—he should be better equipped to take care of someone else. A stronger man would be able to do it and not break a sweat.

Once his grandfather was cleaned up, Dallas moved the back of the chair so that he was sitting upright. He helped the older man change out of his bedclothes and into something suitable for church. His grandfather had a closet full of suits, but he insisted on wearing the red one—the one that Dallas had sewn. It was a little loose, since the last time Andy had felt well enough for service he had been a few sizes larger. Dallas wished that he had time to take it in, but there was too much else to do. No one would notice anyway, he reasoned—and if they did, they would not comment. Wicker was full of gossips, but they were rarely snide to your face.

Andy ran his hand over his hoary cheeks pointedly. Dallas gave him a small smile.

"I haven't forgotten," Dallas said gently. He slid his hand up his grandfather's tie lovingly and made sure that it was entirely straight. "I've got your razor right here."

"The doors open at five o' clock," his grandfather said. "I don't want to be late."

"You won't be," Dallas promised. He picked up the old coffee cup he used to store the disposable razors upside-down before grabbing a can of shaving cream that was almost empty. "And even if you are, I don't think they will hold it against you." He gave another small smile and shot spurts of foam onto his fingers. "I think Reverend Blue would allow you to walk right down the aisle and join the choir in the middle of Amazing Grace."

Andy scoffed softly under his breath, but Dallas could tell that he was pleased. His grandfather took a lot of pride in his presence in the choir—back in the day. Back before everything else.

Once his grandfather's cheeks were shaven, Dallas patted them dry with a hand towel and put everything away. The last thing he did was use a little bit of water and a barber's comb to get his grandfather's plume of white hair all straightened out. By the end of it, Andy may not have looked entirely like his old self—but he was a good bit closer than he had been in a long time.

Finally, his grandfather stood. The leather arms of his chair sank as he pushed his knotted knuckles down into their padding. Dallas held out his hands, ready to catch the older man if he fell. Andy disregarded him almost entirely, grunting and wheezing underneath his breath as he strained every nerve, visibly fighting his body's desire to crumple.

Andy swayed a little, but he finally straightened his back enough to stand. Dallas took a half step back to give him some room, keeping his eyes on his grandfather as he groped the air for the walker that stayed tucked away nearby.

Andy Hackett waved his hand in disgust. "I don't need that," he said. "Reverend Blue said to run."

"But not," Dallas' words were almost a whisper, "literally." He pulled the walker around a little more insistently.

"Delta." His grandfather straightened his back a little more. "You need to have faith." Something that looked like pain twitched across his face. "I will be going forward with gladness in my heart. Whatever may come, there is joy unspeakable—" He clapped his hands together, hitting the ridges of his palms against one another with his gnarled fingers bowed back. "And full of glory! Do you remember the words?"

Dallas nodded, too busy trying to swallow his own dread to join his grandfather in joyous song. Andy took a shaky step forward, followed almost immediately by a more confident stride. He tilted his chin up until his lower jaw strained and the ridges of his crooked bottom teeth stuck out over his top lip. His larynx trembled with the pitch of his untrained tenor as he continued to clap and sing the old gospel hymn. He was dancing towards the door, balancing on the square heels of his worn shoes.

Dallas' fear seized him by the throat and dragged him across the room so quickly that he almost left his cane behind. He grabbed his cane but left his jacket, never once tearing his eyes away from his grandfather's twisting and jolting steps. Andy Hackett danced his way out the door and began his one-man parade down the slick mud streets, arms waving and head wobbling like he was fixing to topple at any minute. Dallas started to pray, clutching the head of his cane as he fought to keep up with his grandfather—who moved as if he was possessed by the Holy Spirit. A miracle if the town had ever seen one.

A few heads poked through their doors and windows at the curious sight. There were whoops and hollers and shouts of 'praise the lord!' that were thrown down like flowers in the path of a Roman emperor. Members of the congregation who were already on their way to church clumped together at this side and joined him in clapping and dancing. It was a sea of red and white that bobbed up and down in joyous waves, and suddenly Dallas wondered if he was the only one who was concerned—or if he was even right to be concerned.

His faith was strong—unwavering, he would even argue. And if his grandfather could muster the strength to dance all the way to church, then why was Dallas limping behind him, leaning on his cane while unable to ignore the throbbing pain embedded in his spine?

The gathering masses came to a stop at the church stoop. The red doors flew open and Reverend Blue stepped out. He smiled broadly and spread his arms at the sight of Andy Hackett, a glorious figure posed like the transfiguration of Christ right there on the top step. Dallas' grandfather stepped forward, and the crowd parted for him. Dallas was close enough to see the tears racing down his grandfather's cheeks as he turned his face up towards Reverend Blue, one trembling arm raised towards the sky—shiny fingers outstretched and seeking absolution.

Reverend Blue grabbed hold of Andy's hand. He began stomping on the church steps as if he were standing behind his pulpit, and he squeezed his eyes shut as his tongue spat out fervent prayers with the ferocity of a cyclone.

"Lord, thank you for bringing our brother Andy back to us today—we know that you can do anything Lord and we are here to praise and worship you—!" His words were echoed by the congregation, who closed in around Dallas' grandfather with outstretched hands, wailing and sobbing as they gripped his clothes and grabbed his shoulder. Reverend Blue pressed his free hand against Andy's forehead and the older man's tears came down faster. They were cloudy, almost white—like pus, like the sickness was draining out of his body.

Dallas stood frozen. He could not move any closer—his only choice was to observe in quiet horror. As soon as they all pulled away, he just knew that his grandfather would fall. All he could picture was his grandfather's head bouncing off the church step and blood matting that white hair. Dallas pressed a hand against his roiling stomach and bent a little at the waist. He could not tear his eyes away— but he wanted, so badly, to leave.

The wailing died down. Snot and tears were running faster than the members of the congregation could fiddle with their little handsewn handkerchiefs and push the corners into their nostrils. One by one they peeled away, until the only person still standing with Andy Hackett was the reverend.

Andy looked like he was already dead. His eyes were wide, glazed over, and fixed forward—but he was not looking at anything. All the color had drained from his face, leaving him pale, with every fold on his sagging cheeks drooping down to his neck. His mouth gaped open slightly, where the pus running from his red-rimmed eyes collected at the corners. His hand rested in the crook of Reverend Blue's elbow where he had been gripping the younger man's forearm, but his hand was slack.

Reverend Blue did not seem to notice. He pushed his palm against Andy's forehead and released his hold at the same time. "In the name of God, Brother Andy, I declare you absolved!"

Andy Hackett fell back as rigid as a board. Dallas screamed and abandoned his cane, throwing himself down to his knees and crawling towards his fallen grandfather. Andy's eyes were staring straight up towards Heaven, but there was nothing left behind them.

Dallas knew he was gone, but that did not stop the ragged cry that tore from his throat. "Help him!" He gripped the front of his grandfather's shirt. "Someone help him, please! God!"

"He's gone, Dallas," Reverend Blue's voice drifted over as a hand landed on Dallas' shoulder. "I'm sorry for your loss. But it is a glad, glad day in Heaven for the son who has been called home."

Dallas pushed his tongue between his teeth and bit down so hard that he tasted blood. It took every ounce of his control not to snarl out words he would regret.

'Fine, but you murdered him. I don't know what you did to him, but this is all your fault, somehow.'

He spat out the unspoken accusation in a glob of bright red snot from the blood on his tongue and the tears that clogged up the back of his palate.

CHAPTER FOUR

AT THE CROSSING

The summer rain had picked up again, slathering the streets and rooftops with long, lazy drizzles. Dallas had lingered long enough to watch the church deacons bicker over what to do with his grandfather's body before finally calling the coroner. After that, he left. He had no desire to attend service. He remembered the long, steady look he had gotten from Reverend Blue before he turned his head and started walking away. The congregation simply acted as though he did not exist. They filed into church, completely obedient—completely unaffected by the man who had dropped dead only seconds before.

Dallas was not actually sure how far out of town he had walked. If he glanced over his shoulder, he could still catch a glimpse of light through the stained-glass church windows, so he reasoned that it was not far enough. He kept walking, happy for once to dwell on the pain in his legs over the agony of his own thoughts. He could not scrub the image of his grandfather's face from his mind—as white as wax, as empty as a cornhusk.

In spite of the rain, he could still see the stars. They were scattered over the weak twilight sky like boils, protruding and glistening as if they could burst at any moment. Dallas could picture easily what it might look like—each star sliding out of its place like a hard cyst, spreading plague where it fell and leaving behind a black, empty pockmark. He wondered what the sky would look like, covered in such seeping holes.

The church got farther and farther behind him until it melted into the thin line of the horizon. Dallas' feet had started to drag a little, and he was relying on his cane to bear more than its usual weight. He came to a stop where one road crossed the other, with the path he was on leading straight into a line of dark trees. The other stretched towards a fuzzy mountain range, only dark lumps behind the curtain of rain—perhaps even at fault for concealing what was left of the sun.

"You are looking mighty troubled, sweet pea." A voice he did not recognize caught his attention and Dallas swung his gaze upward to find the source. It was sweet and carefully cultivated, decidedly masculine but with the cadence that one might assign to an old Southern Belle from a black-and-white flick. "Why don't you sit down for a minute? You look like you've got the whole world on your shoulders."

He felt that way, but Dallas did not want to admit it out loud. He caught sight of a pair of brown eyes, visible even in the encroaching darkness. They were rich umber pools with flecks of orange and green, the same color as wet autumn leaves. Fine lips curled around the pinched end of a gold cigarette holder, while white smoke streamed from the split between their lips in soft, downy clouds.

Dallas licked his lips and pulled his gaze down again, choosing to focus on the stranger's chin instead of their alluring dark eyes or suggestive, curling mouth. He drove his free hand into his pocket and pulled his cane close to his hip.

"Sit?" he asked. The stranger drew their cigarette holder down and slid it through the air. The glowing orange tip of their cigarette drew Dallas' eye towards a beautiful wheelchair sitting in front of them. The whole thing was beyond practical—the frame was sunflower yellow and the seat looked like it was plush leather. It smelled new, even underneath the tobacco and the rain. The spokes on the wheels looked like they had been decked out in chrome. It had all the glamor of a shiny new Corvette.

Suddenly, Dallas was very aware of his own wet clothing, He shook his head.

"I don't want to ruin it," he said.

"You won't," the stranger reassured him. They brought their cigarette holder back to their lips. "Although it makes no difference to me, whether you use it or not."

Dallas hesitated for only a second longer. He took them up on the offer and sat down. The seat was miraculously dry and unbelievably comfortable. The relief in his aching back was instantaneous.

"There. Not so bad, now, is it?" The stranger tilted their head. "You're quite a ways from the church doors."

"I can't seem to get far enough." Dallas tried not to get choked up again, but he was losing the battle. "I don't think I can go back."

"Why not?" The question drifted on a ribbon of smoke.

"Because..." Dallas swallowed. "I might hurt someone, if I do."

"Oh?" The stranger's voice sheltered a secret smile. "How would you do that?"

"I don't know," Dallas admitted. He rubbed his hands up and down the padded arms of the new wheelchair. "Maybe I would shut everyone inside, lock the doors, and set it on fire."

"That is one way to do things," the stranger said.

"It's terrible to even think." Dallas sawed at his bottom lip. The rain was slacking off at last, and the sun had set completely. The sky was jet black and the stars were brighter than ever.

"Why?" the stranger prodded. "Don't they deserve it?"

"They killed my grandfather." Dallas closed his eyes and tightened his grip on the wheelchair. "I know that sounds crazy. You probably wouldn't believe me if I told you how it happened."

"Try me," the stranger urged.

"There is something not right," Dallas said. "Something not normal. And maybe I am a terrible believer. Maybe it was a test of faith, and I failed."

The stranger moved a little closer and brushed their hand over Dallas' cheek. He shivered and opened his eyes, looking back up at them.

"Maybe," the stranger said. "Or maybe it is as you say, and they deserve to go up in a blaze."

Dallas shivered. "I don't know," he said. "I don't know—I think it is me. I think I should go back and talk to the reverend."

"Dallas," the stranger interrupted firmly. The sound of the name he had not given was like a shot to the gut and Dallas sat upright, now too afraid to protest. "What do you want most, in the world?"

Dallas went quiet. No one had ever asked him that before. He tried to think about it, but all he could see was his grandfather's waxy dead face.

"I want them to suffer," he said. "The whole congregation. I need them to pay for what they did, and the reverend. All of them. No one else will hold them accountable if not me."

"Easy enough," the stranger said. "I believe that we can come to some arrangement on that."

Dallas furrowed his brow. "I'm not sure what you mean," he said. "I'm here babbling nonsense—vile, awful sort of fantasies and all you can say is 'that can be arranged'. Do I want to know how? I don't even know your name."

The stranger smiled. "My friends call me Abel," they said. "I think you and I will be very good friends, Dallas, so you can call me by that name. And I think you know what I am, you just cannot bring yourself to accept it. You believe in God, but do you believe in the Devil as well?"

"Of course I do," Dallas' words escaped quickly. "I believe in all of it. God, the Devil, the whole nine. Are you him? Are you Satan?"

"Something along those lines." Abel drew their smoke trails into a little cloudy heart. "Let's just say I would not be very welcome on Sunday morning."

Suddenly, Dallas was not afraid, even though he knew that he should be. He found himself seeking out Abel's brown eyes again, simply for the comfort of their warmth. "All right," he said, accepting it all in one radical sweep. "What can you do for me?" His voice quivered. It all felt like a betrayal. A dirty, rotten move like swiping candy from the counter while the grocer was still watching. All while knowing that no one was going to come after you—you were free to enjoy the candy, but it was the sin of it—and the lack of remorse.

It was not too late, in theory. He could still run to Reverend Blue and ask for prayer and God's forgiveness. Absolution, a benison—he still had a home, after all, even if it was empty.

Abel's words pulled him back. "I can give you strength," the devil said. "I can be your helping hand."

When phrased in that way, it sounded so perfectly reasonable. Through his muddled, grieving thoughts, Dallas could not think of one reason to turn it down. And it was not as if this fiend was saying, 'I can kill them all for you'. It was a leg-up, if anything, the choices were all still his.

"What is your price?" Dallas managed to get enough of his head together to ask. "What do I give you in exchange?"

Abel crouched until they were level with Dallas' chair and held his gaze, resting their gentle hand on top of his.

"I will collect my due in flesh," Abel said. "On every new moon, your body will be entirely at my disposal." They stroked Dallas' knuckles. "A piddling price tag for an invaluable service."

Was that all? Dallas drew in a breath. "Every new moon until when?"

Abel shrugged. "As long as you need me." Their smile, for a moment, looked more hungry than placating. "So, presumably, for the rest of your life."

Was that the real method of soul collection? Inch by inch, measured in flesh sinking into flesh, harvested from a platter formed by sin-bearing hips and scraped up by demanding claws? Were shattered pieces of the damned glued together by heated tongues, melted down like hunks of wax into formless shapes until they no longer resembled the people they once were?

The rest of his life—it could be three more years or sixty. An indefinite promise for an ambiguous reward.

"All right," Dallas said at last. In that moment he felt entirely separate from his body—caught somewhere in-between observation and action. "What do I need to do?"

The devil wove their fingers through Dallas' and clasped his hand, using the grip to draw it close to their mouth and press their lips against his knuckles.

"Allow me to walk back with you," they said. "I can push your wheelchair."

Dallas nodded with his words frozen on his tongue.

CHAPTER FIVE

WHEN THE ROLL IS CALLED UP YONDER

The house was unnervingly silent, and all the lights were still on inside. Through the thin yellow curtains, Dallas could just see the outline of his grandfather's abandoned recliner, and it made him sick.

The devil was still behind him, keeping faithful vigilance at the handles of the wheelchair. Abel had been quiet for most of their walk, allowing Dallas plenty of time to stew over his decision. An unwelcome dose of regret tried to throw itself forward and he brushed it away. There was no time for that.

Abel pushed him up the narrow walkway that led up to the front steps and then paused. There was no ramp in either the front or the back—which was something Dallas had not considered. He dreaded getting out of his new wheelchair to walk up the steps. His legs and back were so stiff that he was not entirely sure he could stand up without assistance. He braced himself against the arms, ready to give it a try, but Abel's hand on his shoulder bid him to sit down.

"There aren't that many steps," the devil said. "I will pop you up. Are you ready?"

Dallas tightened his grip on the wheelchair's arms and nodded. Abel rolled the chair back about an inch and then popped the front wheels up. Dallas' entire world tilted and he squeezed the leather arms, digging his fingernails into the padded sides while Abel set the wheels against the step and pushed him up towards the front door.

"Would you like a bath?" Abel asked once the wheels had clattered over the threshold. "I can draw one up for you."

"Yes, please," Dallas said. "I can draw it myself, though." He tilted his head back to glance up. "I did not expect you to be kind."

"It is not true kindness." Abel locked the chair's brakes once they were settled in the living room. "It is not selfless by any means."

Dallas shrugged. He pushed his toes against the footrests to lift them up so he could step out of the chair. His back screamed and he hissed in pain, rotating as quickly as he could to land in his grandfather's leather chair. It rocked a bit with his sudden weight and the seat sank down past the arms. It smelled like piss and must, and he did not dare touch his face against the thin blanket that had been thrown over the back.

"Here." Abel produced Dallas' cane, which he had forgotten about until that moment. The devil propped it up against the nearby side table. "I will return."

Dallas could only nod as his eyelids began to sink against his will. Exhaustion held hands with his pain and darkness drew in from the corners of his vision while the flesh around his swollen knees felt too tight to bend. His head drooped down until it was resting against the arm of the recliner, and he managed to pull his legs up into the seat enough to curl and relieve his back.

Somewhere, water was gushing from a faucet. The sound trickled into his dreams, and he dreamt that he was drowning.

Sunlight pierced the mustard-colored curtains and soaked the entire living room in diseased yellow. Dallas threw his arm over his eyes and pushed his face into the arm of the leather chair. He did not even remember falling asleep, and it took a solid minute for him to recollect entirely what had happened the night before. Despair burrowed into his gut and he drew his knees closer to his chest. Suddenly, it was impossible to move. He had no desire to get up out of the chair, even though his throat was dry and his clothes were still damp.

"Abel?" he called out tentatively. There was no answer. It was possible that he had dreamt up the pretty devil and their smoldering brown eyes with soft orange lights like sparks.

"Dallas?" A more familiar voice called from the front door. Dallas sat up immediately, clamping his hand down on the back of his neck to try and work out the kinks.

"Reverend?" he called back. He cleared his throat and adjusted his position in the chair. His leg slid out and he banged his foot against the wheelchair that was sitting close by. Dallas shredded an expletive through his teeth and leaned over to push the wheelchair away.

Not a dream, after all—but then where had the devil gone?

Reverend Blue appeared in the living room entrance. He was wearing a plain, long-sleeved red shirt and straight white trousers without a crease or a speck of dirt. His blonde hair gleamed with the same expensive shine as the gold-and-pearl cross earring dangling from his right ear.

"There you are." Blue swept his wide-brimmed black hat away from his head. "Forgive my intrusion. You gave us quite a scare last night."

Dallas bit a tab of dry skin on his bottom lip. "I gave you a scare?" he asked.

"Running out of town like that." Reverend Blue shook his head. "Your grandfather has been with Mr. Richter at the morgue, waiting for you to identify him proper so we can give him a burial."

"Why does the morgue need me to identify him?" Dallas shot back. "Everyone here knew him."

"You're his only kin," Blue said. He glanced around and then gestured to the green velvet chair that was nearby.

"May I sit?" He did so without waiting for a response. Dallas' eyes stung, and he ground his fingers into them to try and alleviate the burn.

"Is that why you came down here?" Dallas asked. "To drag me to the morgue?"

"Dallas." The reverend's voice softened. "I am not here to drag you anywhere. If you want someone to escort you there, I would be mighty proud to do so. Otherwise..." He threw another look around. "There is something else I wanted to discuss."

And there it was. Dallas raised his chin and dug his fingers into the side of his thigh. He wished that he had not fallen asleep. The smell of his damp, unwashed clothes was starting to get to him.

"And what is that?" he asked. He had his theories. His grandfather had it written in his will that ten percent of all he owned was to be turned over to the church upon his death. Andy Hackett had died without much of anything to his name, but there was still the house—and an old Dodge truck that did not run, but it was probably worth something. It was within the church's power to send an appraiser through to see what of the dead man's belongings could be salvaged. They would probably take the house, too, and try to divide the earnings. Dallas had seen it happen too many times. The Church of New Lazarus was ruthless when it came to collecting its due—and with its fingers firmly pressed against the pulse of Wicker's throat, it could do anything it liked.

There were too many families—widows, children, grandchildren—who had been stripped of every penny and buried in debt by funeral expenses. Now they lived and ate off the church's charity.

Dallas was loyal, but he would go down fighting like an animal before anyone took his grandfather's house.

"God spoke to me in a dream last night," Reverend Blue said. Even as he spoke, he held up his hands—manicured nails shining like glass. "He appeared to me as a column of fire and commanded me to take off my shoes, for the ground I walked upon was consecrated. I obeyed, ripping them off my feet and casting them aside. I fell to my knees, but the Lord bid me to rise. He called me closer to the flame, where I was afraid to walk because I did not want to burn. Even so, I obeyed. As I got closer to the flames, I realized that they were cool, and that I could run my fingers through their tongues as easily as if they were ripples in a creek. Then, in the very center of the column, I saw a face—a blazing white angel holding a sword. The fire licking the blade had turned blue, and when the angel opened their mouth, their voice was as pure as a child's. I almost cried, I was so overcome. But then the angel spoke, and they told me that I had a sacred duty to fulfill. As the shepherd of my congregation, I am burdened by the weight of their sorrows. If I could alleviate the suffering of every single body and soul that settles into my pews on Sunday mornings, I would. However, I am still only a man—but the Lord has brought me your suffering, Dallas, and has told me how I might relieve you of your grief."

The more he spoke, the more Dallas' uncertainty made its way through the tight walls of his intestines and cramped painfully. Dallas pressed his hand against his belly and tried not to shift too much, not wanting to look as nervous as he felt.

"What did the Lord say?" Dallas asked. He wanted to doubt it—even the most stalwart believer would have trouble swallowing every detail of such a vision, in his opinion. Yet, after the encounter he had on the crossroads—he realized that he did not have any business doubting the reverend.

"The Lord spoke in many tongues old and new—and somehow I was able to understand them," Reverend Blue said. "He told me that I am to help you in every way. That I am to open my arms and bring you closer to the church. To not let you stray, to keep you safe—and he said that the best way to do all this is by the sacred ritual of spiritual matrimony."

If the reverend had stood up and struck Dallas across the face, he would not have been more stunned. Dallas sat there and stared at him, waiting for the punchline as if the reverend was about to step back and reveal everything to be some sort of grand joke. Yet, Reverend Blue did not pull his eyes away. He kept them fixed on Dallas, unwavering and calm.

It was the first time Dallas realized that Reverend Blue's smile did not touch his eyes. And judging from the lack of fine lines lurking around the corners, it never did.

"I can't marry you," Dallas said dumbly. "I am..." 'a boy', he thought, but then it dawned on him, 'not really'. Legally, he did not have the right parts that would stamp the coveted 'M' on his birth certificate. Legally, there was nothing stopping them. "What would the congregation think?" he blurted out. "A man. A cripple. Is that the sort of spiritual partner God wants for you?" He dug his nails into his bottom lip, ripping up chunks of skin until the blood started to stain his fingertips.

"I am not here to question the commands of the Lord." Reverend Blue's voice took on a severe gravity. "Nor will I tolerate arguments against His will." He leaned forward. "You are alone in this world, Dallas Hackett, but God does not want you to feel alone. He knows that you will stray if you are not looked after, and as your shepherd, it is my duty to mind you. There is no greater honor. Your grandfather would have seen that."

Dallas wished desperately for something—someone—to intervene. His thoughts strayed again to Abel, wondering where they had gone, hoping that if he managed to delay things long enough they would walk through the front door and put an end to this nightmarish conversation.

Marry Reverend Blue. Marry Reverend Blessing Easton of the Church of New Lazarus.

Give up his grandfather's house. Give everything to God.

Only twelve hours before, if that, he had promised his body to the devil. Now, God was demanding him to serve as the reverend's fuck toy.

Another patch of dry skin peeled off his lip and blood crusted underneath his nail. Dallas dashed his tongue over the fresh battle wounds, relishing and taking comfort in their sting.

"I am no one," Dallas finally said. "I cannot question the word of God."

Reverend Blue smiled and showed off all his even white teeth. He took Dallas' hand in his own and pulled it towards him, stroking the young man's knuckles.

"Somehow," the reverend said, "I feel I should have known that this was what God intended from the start. From the moment I saw you, I could not look away. You were crowned in glory—with hair like the very fires from which God spoke to me. It was a message, I understand that now. I was blind, but now I see. Bless the Lord."

"O, my soul." Dallas felt like he was in danger of throwing up, even though there was nothing on his stomach.

"We will have to tell the congregation," Reverend Blue said. "But before we go—will you indulge me?"

Dallas nodded and the reverend gripped his hand a little tighter.

"I think we should pray," he said, "and thank God that He has brought us together. Here, in this moment, we are His true and faithful servants."

Dallas could only nod again. He bowed his head, but even as Reverend Blue launched into prayer, he could not focus on the words that were being said.

He kept looking around for any sign of his true salvation, but the devil was still nowhere to be seen.

CHAPTER SIX

BLESSED ASSURANCE

When small town folk weren't taking communion, gossip was all they had to chew on. Rumors regarding Dallas and the reverend's planned spiritual union spread like a bushfire. There were very few who approved—especially those who had known Dallas since he was still in pigtails.

Marge Elsie had been very vocal about it, for her part. She did not say anything to the reverend's face, but Dallas caught plenty of snatches from her hen-pecking session during his grandfather's funeral reception. She sat in a corner surrounded by several other of the church's most esteemed ladies. Their large, flowery hats bobbed up and down with agreement while she made her opinions well-known from behind the round, crinkled edges of a paper fan.

Dallas only caught a bit of what she had to say.

"—Mind you, it is not because she—he—started off life as a little girl," Marge Elsie said. "I am not a prejudiced woman and I believe that God has the final say in all things. When Andy told me that Delta had come to him wanting to be a man, well, you know I had a hard time wrapping my mind around it. But I told him, 'Andy, God has a plan for your little Delta. Don't give up on her.' And by the Lord's grace, he never did. Not until the day he died. But it's one thing to wear a man's clothes and it's another thing to act on the sins of Sodomy. I believe that our reverend is being tempted by the Evil One. Amen."

"Sister Marge Elsie," another woman, Rebecca, whispered. "Can women commit the sin of Sodomy? I thought that was only men who—you know."

Marge Elise gave her a withering look. "Sister Rebecca, whether it is cocks or cunts—forgive my language but the Lord knows my heart—it is Sodomy if there is penetration of the unholy variety."

A few of the church women gasped. Marge Elsie nodded sagely.

"Anything beyond the act of missionary," she said knowledgably. "It is called missionary for a reason— Amen—because anything else is an act of the devil."

She caught sight of Dallas, at that point, and went stone silent. Dallas forced himself to meet her eyes and sipped lemonade from the brim of his paper cup.

The church's reception hall was just a second trailer only a few steps away from the main one that served as their sanctuary. It still had the kitchen installed, peeling linoleum and all, where the old biddies had gathered at six in the morning before service to prepare hot fried chicken with all the fixin's. Nothing buried grief better than a heap of gravy-smothered mashed potatoes and macaroni salad. And church folks couldn't plan around anything unless lunch was attached.

Reverend Blue flitted through the dining areas, which were just the individual rooms of the trailer filled with card tables instead of real furniture. He carried his plate around, cooing over the old ladies' cooking and touching the heads of small children with a fraternal style of affection. Blue just had that way about him—community leader to the bone. It was in the way he bounced his leg and moved his hands when he got excited, as if he was so full of the Holy Spirit that glory was leaking out from every pore. Dallas followed him silently, aware that he should start performing that role he would soon enough fill. It was hard to feign enthusiasm when he did not feel it—much less take Blue's seriously, when he had gotten close enough to see edges of the mask.

Thankfully, no one really spoke to Dallas, unless it was to offer condolences or say something about how much they loved his grandfather. Even though Andy had not been part of the congregation properly in years, they all remembered his singing, his smile, and his generous bear hugs. An eternal member of the choir. They would hang a plaque for him on the wall. And so it went. Dallas could offer nothing in return other than a small smile and a quiet 'thank you'. He was tired of people grabbing his hand and kneading his fingers. He was tired of people pulling him into their arms and patting him solidly on the back. Every bit of it felt insincere—not for his grandfather, but for him.

He wondered how many of them would have gladly traded his life for his grandfather's. One crippled queer for a man of God who donated generously to their causes. A few more years for Andy Hackett were far more valuable on the balanced scale than decades, even a lifetime, for Dallas.

Blue stopped his rounds at the dessert table and lingered there. He folded his paper plate in half and dropped it into the trash with most of his food still on it.

"Is something on your mind, Dallas?" he asked. He turned his head and extended his hand while he spoke. Despite everything Dallas had turned over in his head about the reverend in the past twenty-four hours, he could not deny that Blue still radiated warmth like a cozy brazier on a crisp autumn night. Dallas ached to give him his hand and allow himself to be pulled close. It was a foreign idea, to be held tight by the Voice of God, but something about Blue made him want it.

Dallas slipped his tongue over his bottom lip. "I keep thinking about my grandfather," he said. "That is all."

Blue nodded sympathetically. "I'm sure it is all still strange for you," he said. "And being around all these people who knew him and loved him must be equal parts a comfort and a sorrow."

"More like a blight." Dallas cast a look around. "It's a strange feeling, but it is like they all wish I was dead, too."

"People have strange ways of expressing their grief," Blue said.

"I don't think they're very keen on the idea of us getting married, either," Dallas added. "Spiritually or otherwise."

"It is God's will," Blue said. "Whether they agree with it or not. You and I are just His servants, and we must follow His command."

"I know." Dallas rubbed his arm. An awkward silence settled in the space between them, shuffling around the distant din of laughter and clattering plasticware.

"Hey." Blue interrupted his thoughts again. Dallas turned his head and let up on his grip. He had not realized how hard was squeezing his own arm.

"Hm?" Dallas tilted his head.

"Have you ever seen the parish?" Blue asked. Dallas furrowed his brow.

"I've walked by plenty of times," he said. The parish was a single-story brick home with a white porch that wrapped around the front and held up a matching swing. Lionel Barry, the church contractor, had replaced the roof the day Reverend Blue came to town.

From the moment Blue set foot on Wicker soil, everyone had just been scrambling to serve him.

"No, no." Reverend Blue waved his hand. "Have you seen it from the inside?"

Dallas shook his head. "Can't say that I have," he said.

"We will have to fix that," Reverend Blue said. "It is going to be your home as well, after all." He extended his hand to Dallas. "Come and see."

His words tugged on a thread of fear that Dallas could not explain. However, he was in no position to refuse.

Dallas slipped his hand into the reverend's, and they walked out with their fingers intertwined.

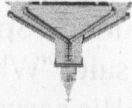

Reverend Blue's single level home rested at the top of a hill and at the end of a straight and narrow driveway. His white front porch posts gleamed like the marble columns of a Greek temple and he stood between them, Zeus somehow descended onto Mt. Sinai. Entering the house felt like a sacred action, what should have been met by a thick cloud of incense and blazing candles around painted icons. There was none of that, however. The only candle that burned was balsam and cedar, and it sat in a glass container in the middle of a squat coffee table.

The house was simple and neat as a pin. Dallas was not sure what else he might have expected. All the furniture had been donated by the congregation, so none of it matched. He recognized a fabric chair that his grandfather had unloaded and a couch that had belonged to a different reverend altogether. Blue left his shoes by the door and walked across the plush red carpet in his black dress socks. Dallas copied his motions, kicking off his worn shoes and tucking them close to the wall.

"It is a nice place," Dallas said. "Very clean." He took another look around.

Blue smiled. "I don't do any of the upkeeping," he said. "Sister Marge Elsie comes over once a week and tidies up. God bless her. I hate to think what this place would look like if not for her."

"The perks to being a reverend, I suppose," Dallas said. He hesitated before he spoke again. "Everyone adores you."

"I don't think that's exactly true." Blue said as he walked towards the kitchen. "Do you want some iced tea? Soda?"

"What do you have?" Without those knowing eyes following him around, Dallas took the liberty of exploring. The nearest door to him was slightly ajar, and all it took was a nudge from his cane to swing open.

"Cream soda, root beer," Blue said. "Ginger ale. Grape…"

"Grape," Dallas replied faintly. He could only assume that he was looking into the reverend's bedroom. The red carpet stretched all the way inside, and the bed was covered in red, too. It was high off the ground and double the size of Dallas' bed at home. The frame itself was massive and carved out of dark wood, with four posts that reached up towards the ceiling in dizzying spirals. Nothing else in the room was quite as impressive or commanded so much attention.

The cold side of a glass bottle nudged his shoulder and Dallas turned his head. He accepted it sheepishly and tried to take a step back, but he ended up stepping on the reverend's foot and nearly toppling backwards into his chest.

"I am sorry," Dallas breathed. Blue reached out to steady him, setting a hand on his waist.

"You have nothing to apologize for," the reverend said. "It is your bed, too."

Dallas nearly choked on a mouthful of grape soda.

"Not yet," he managed after clearing his throat. "And I…"

"And you…?" Blue took a swig out of his own bottle.

"Well." Dallas looked at the bed again. "It does set up…pretty high expectations."

Blue laughed. Dallas could not tell whether it was genuine, but the sound sent pins and needles all the way down to his toes.

"Does it?" Blue asked. "I never thought of it that way. It was here when I arrived." He reached underneath Dallas' arm to grab the door handle and pulled it closed. "If it helps you to know, the state of the bed does not reflect my own anticipations."

Dallas swallowed. "The only thing I would have to say, if it did, is that you might be disappointed." He turned until he was facing the reverend, his own heaving chest pressed up against the taller man's. Blue's chest was still—his whole body was still. Dallas could not even feel the reverend's heartbeat past the racing muscle behind his own ribs.

"I don't think so," Blue said. He slid his eyes up and down Dallas' form, taking it all in leisurely. He slipped his hand through the air, circling the shape of Dallas' ear and only coming close enough to touch the very end of a corkscrewed copper curl. The curl landed against his jaw, and Dallas felt the reverend's fingertips graze the bone. Every nerve lit up, and a shiver took over Dallas' body, rocking him on his feet.

Dallas dropped his cane. He placed his hands against the reverend's chest while Blue's arm tightened around his waist, pulling him even closer. Underneath the strong balsam and cedar candle, the reverend smelled like where he had been. A splash of Aqua Velva on top of musty church carpet and simmering barbecue.

"Forgive me," Dallas whispered. He had to scrape every word out of his throat. "I..." He lifted his hands so that they were no longer touching the reverend's chest. "I dropped my cane."

"I saw," Blue said. "I will pick it up for you." He moved his fingers down the hard line of Dallas' jaw, trailing them through the air once again before coming to rest underneath his chin. He tilted Dallas' head up until their eyes were forced to meet. Blue's lilac eyes were empty without a drop of warmth to make the color spark. His whole face was like a painting—all resemblance, no life. And yet he smiled, and his lips curved in a charming way. They were like the red gumdrops that used to tantalize Dallas from his grandmother's candy dish.

"Are you pure, Dallas Hackett?" Reverend Blue asked. It was not the question that Dallas had been expecting, for some reason. He stumbled over it for too long before he finally answered.

"There is none pure in this world," Dallas stammered. "We are all sinners."

"Yes," Reverend Blue said. "But that is not what I am asking. Not in spirit, but in body—are you pure?"

Dallas swallowed. "Yes," he said. Even as the word slipped out, he could not help but feel as though it were a lie. He supposed that it was not—he had never had sex, and he knew that that was what the reverend was asking. However, he had touched himself plenty. He had taken his pleasure into his own hands once or twice using whatever he could find. His favorite toy had been a handheld back massager that he had stolen from a drawer. He missed it, thinking about it.

The reverend seemed neither approving nor disapproving. "Are you curious?" He took the bottle from

Dallas' hand, setting it and his own on a nearby table. "Are you afraid?"

'Yes,' Dallas wanted to say. "I am not afraid of you," he said aloud, although that was not true either.

"Good," Blue said. "I don't want you to be." His words skated over Dallas' skin as he lowered his face until their lips were nearly touching. "Have you ever been kissed?"

Dallas looked up at him through gingery lashes. "No," he said. He didn't think that one boy behind the schoolhouse in second grade counted. And he didn't think Blue would, either.

Blue stroked underneath Dallas' chin, starting his fingers at his throat and trailing them up. "Would you like me to kiss you now?" he asked.

Dallas wrapped his hand around Blue's but he did not move it. He stroked the reverend's fingers and pressed his hips even closer, since they were the only part of him not completely adhered to Blue's body already.

"Uh huh," Dallas finally nodded. Intelligent words failed him, and he decided that they were wasted in the moment anyway. He pushed himself up onto his toes and pressed his lips against Blue's, clasping the back of the reverend's head and pulling him down into a heated kiss.

CHAPTER SEVEN

HOW FIRM A FOUNDATION

Dallas pressed his tongue against Blue's lips and they broke apart at the contact. Blue opened his mouth for the intrusion, bracing his hands against Dallas' back in an effort to keep them both steady. Blue's mouth was hot and his tongue was bigger, longer. After a moment he pushed back against Dallas' tongue and Dallas pushed back, fighting for control as he wound his fingers through the reverend's short blonde hair.

Blue staggered back. His back hit the wall and Dallas pressed into him, merciless in his pursuit. He ground his hips against the reverend's with deranged fervor, seized by the desire to get as close as he could—no matter what it took. In that moment, he felt like he could tear open the reverend's chest and climb inside—if only he could get past his shirt. He wanted Blue's hands to move lower, to wander from his back to his ass. He wanted Blue to grip him in all the tight, wet places and throw him down onto the ground and show him the wrath of the Almighty.

The feeling terrified him. Dallas had no idea where it came from. It was like some beast lurking inside that had been sprung free by Reverend Blue's words. Or maybe it had been the closeness of his body, lingering too long like a match to a wick. Dallas was suddenly possessed, hungry, burning.

Every damning word that could ever be uttered against a sinner consumed by lust spun around his head. It did not stop him from reaching out and grabbing between the reverend's legs. He clamped his fingers around something thick and firm, although Reverend Blue's hand pulled his away so quickly that he did not have time to explore.

"Not yet," Blue said, his voice strained. "Not yet. We need to wait."

Dallas had to fight to squeeze out a reply. "You act as though it is all mine, already," he said. "Is this not why you brought me here?"

Blue shook his head. "It needs to be..." Before he could finish, he captured Dallas' mouth in another kiss. He tightened his grip on the young man's waist and pushed against him to flip him around. He pressed Dallas' back against the wall and ground against him, drawing up his knee to split apart the other man's thighs. Dallas wrapped himself around the reverend's leg and squeezed, sliding up and down as fiery need made every stroke feel divine.

Dallas was wet enough that he could feel his pants sticking to his hot slick skin, and every jolt from bouncing his hips against the reverend's leg made his cunt ache in a deep, needy way that could not be satisfied by a simple rub-out. Still, he was going to take what he could get. He tried to use his hand to stimulate the reverend in turn, but Blue caught him by the wrists and held him close, kissing and moving his leg up and down while Dallas ground against it until helpless whimpers started spilling out of his throat. They were followed by heady moans that dribbled off his tongue like senseless prayers.

Tension built between Dallas' thighs, tightening in his ass and winding around his spine like a metal coil. His entire body felt tighter than a spring, and he leaned his head back to try and focus on the warmth and the building ache. His breath came out in short, hard gasps while Blue's mouth pressed against his windpipe. Dallas swallowed and felt the swell push against the reverend's lips. His whole body quaked. Blue's hands still held his wrists in place and even Dallas' fingers ached from being bent in their tense curled position.

Dallas felt it—although he was not sure what it was—he could tell that he was close. He whimpered again and threw his head forward, burying it in Blue's neck and inhaling the reverend's deeper scent. Underneath his cologne, his soap, his skin, his sweat. Dallas dragged his tongue over the reverend's throbbing pulse and drew the skin into his mouth, sucking.

Reverend Blue jerked his head back and pulled his leg away. A frustrated cry tore out of Dallas' throat and he nearly collapsed. He propped himself up against the wall and shot Blue a glare—as heated a look as he had ever dared give the reverend. Blue returned it with a scathing one of his own, and dash of disapproving blue that quickly doused Dallas' flaring temper.

"I must ask that you not leave marks," Reverend Blue said tersely. He pressed his hand against his neck and rubbed the side that Dallas had latched onto. "Especially when we are combatting the whispers of the entire congregation."

Dallas let out a shaky breath and nodded his head. "Forgive me," he said. His wits were still swimming around his head, but he managed to straighten and smooth out the front of his suit.

His red pants were dark between his legs and soaked through. He could smell his own heat and need.

"We should return." Blue swiped his fingers down the corners of his mouth. There were beads of sweat there and on his forehead. His whole face glistened like it had been dipped in oil. "Everyone will be making their way to the interment site soon."

Of course. In the heat of it all, Dallas had forgotten about everything else. He had forgotten entirely about his grandfather. A spike of guilt speared him so deeply in the gut that what little lunch he had eaten threatened to come up.

"I feel..." He did not have words for how he felt. 'Sick' was not all-encompassing enough. Blue seemed to understand. He granted Dallas a look of sympathetic severity and set a hand on his shoulder, giving it a squeeze.

"Come on," Blue said. "We will walk back together."

Dallas' grandfather was buried in the oldest graveyard in Wicker. It shared a fence line with a peach grove and some of the overripe, pale fruits had fallen onto the dead's side to rot against the same soil. Andy Hackett had loved peach preserves. There was a run of several years where he had boiled and canned his own and passed them out to the ladies in church for Christmas baskets. A little taste of summer in the dead of winter, he would say.

Dallas caught himself straying from the graveside while Blue preached. He couldn't keep his mind on the sermon, anyway. Everyone was tired. It was high noon, and their bellies were full. More than a few of the church ladies could be seen hiking up their skirts to try and discreetly scratch an itch through their thick pantyhose, and the pallbearers were starting to nod off. Their heads bobbed up and down like goslings on a lake. It seemed to Dallas like there was only so much inspiring the Holy Spirit could do.

The graveyard was small, so he could still hear Blue as he walked. Dallas stepped over grave markers and darted around headstones, muttering apologies under his breath as though he were dodging elbows in a crowd. The dirt closest to the fence was downright cold under the heavy shade. A few fat, fallen peaches rested half-buried in the dirt or collapsed against raised roots with their fuzzy skins wrinkled from their seeping insides. Dallas sat down cross-legged in the dirt and picked up one of the peaches, rolling it around in his hands and pushing the loose skin around with his thumbs. It slid easily and bunched up wherever it was shoved, just like the skin around his grandfather's neck. Dallas pursed his lips and pushed his thumbs deeper into the peach. The gushing flesh caved underneath the pressure and kept the impressions of his thumbs even when he pulled them away. Dallas passed the peach from hand to hand and then closed his fingers around it again, holding it against his nose to take in the sweetly sour smell of rotting fruit and earth.

Dallas wanted to think more about his grandfather. It felt wrong not to, after all. Yet, in that moment, all he could hear was Blue's voice. It smothered every other sound, just like all he could think about was the reverend's face. He liked how it had been hot and flushed, with just one rebellious strand of blonde hair coming free from its perfectly gelled coif. Dallas wondered if the reverend knew that he had a very craggy purple vein that stuck out across his temple. Dallas wanted to trace it with his tongue just to feel the hard pulse against the tip. It was equally as hard to forget about how Blue had squirmed away when Dallas latched onto his neck. Animal instinct made Dallas want to pin him down to the floor and tear into his flesh with his teeth. If only the reverend had not handled him so effectively.

Dallas discarded the peach he was holding and picked up another. It had a firmer skin but a rotten spot. The ugly black spread from the creased center and over the fruit's misshapen hump. It oozed clear fluid and reeked of tooth-rottingly sweet peach. Dallas kept his grip on the fruit and braced his cane against the dirt to stand. His legs had been shaking before he sat down, and he was not looking forward to walking home after the graveside service ended.

A yellow-gloved hand descended across his vision. Elegant fingers uncurled and reached towards him in an unspoken offer. The gloves were shiny, soft-looking leather and only covered half the wearer's hand. Dallas did not take it immediately. He raised his head and locked eyes with the devil, who was standing on a bulging root and looming over him expectantly, hand still extended and unwavering. The devil cast no shadow—or perhaps it was just because they were standing in the shade of the peach tree.

"Why aren't you using your chair?" the devil asked glibly. Dallas made a face.

"The cemetery is a little hilly," he said, looking over his shoulder. "And it just felt like—a lot."

Abel quirked a fine eyebrow. "Sure," they said. "But it is no good to you sitting at home."

"I just didn't like the idea of making the reverend help me," Dallas said. "It seemed—wrong."

"Isn't the reverend going to be your husband?" Abel's eyes slid over to where the reverend was standing. "Why, he's almost got one foot in the grave already."

Dallas sucked on his teeth. "That isn't funny."

"If he is going to marry you, then he needs to get used to helping you around." The devil tucked a lock of brown hair behind their ear and pulled out a long gold cigarette holder from behind it. From their pocket they produced a matching gold cigarette case with an elaborate letter "H" etched in ivory on the lid. "You wanted them all to pay, didn't you? Well, there he is. One little shove and you could send him on over to the pearly gates." They smiled a bit at that, as if remembering an inside joke.

"Oh, yeah," Dallas scoffed quietly. "And everyone else standing around over there would send me over with him."

Abel shrugged and selected a cigarette to slide into the holder. "People like that—you just have to win them over. I think you're more capable than you realize."

Dallas turned the peach around in his hands and swiped his thumbs over the rotten spot. "I stick out," he said. He held up the peach to illustrate his point further. "Would you bite into something that looked like this and trust it not to make you sick?"

Abel paused to light the end of their cigarette and take in the first draw. Smoke curled from their nostrils and flooded the separation of their plush pink mouth. "Do you know anything about cuckoo birds?"

Dallas pulled the peach back down to his lap and huffed. "No," he said. He began gouging out the slimy black pieces from the side of the peach and flicking them off the ends of his fingers.

"The way they work is that they lay their eggs in the nests of other birds," Abel explained. "The egg will look like a copy of the others, and so the host bird will care for it as her own. After the egg hatches, the cuckoo chick will push the host bird's eggs out of the nest. It will push out the other hatchlings, too." Abel took another drag off their cigarette. "It is instinct on the chick's part, so that it can have all the food for itself."

"Then they're parasites," Dallas said flatly. He flung another chunk of rotting fruit to the ground.

"I find it fascinating," Abel responded. "To thrive so strongly without ever doing any of the nurturing." The devil rested one hand against their hip as they watched the graveside service wind down. "Not to mention, they mate with multiple partners in a single season."

Dallas grabbed his cane and stood up, still clutching the decimated peach in one hand. He swung around to face the grave, standing beside Abel who was so still and perfectly poised in the late afternoon sun.

"I think your man is ready for you," the devil said.

"Another thing about cuckoo birds," Dallas said. "It sounds like they are happy to abandon their chicks. So the parent flees, and the hatchling has to fend for itself."

He turned his head to get Abel's thoughts, but the devil had already vanished.

CHAPTER EIGHT

CROWN HIM WITH MANY CROWNS

What it really came down to, Dallas was starting to realize, was the matter of who would officiate the wedding. Blue could not very well do it, and there was a great deal of debate amongst the deacons about who could—seeing as how any reverend brought in would have to be from the same denomination, and the Church of New Lazarus was the first of its kind. No one else really came close to the doctrine that Reverend Blue and his followers subscribed to. Donnie Ray, one of the younger deacons, offered to call in a favor from his cousin down in Birmingham. He pitched this cousin as a real down-to-earth fella without a bit of nonsense about his character.

"Been a preacher of ten years now, and he would be mighty glad to do it. Not a penny out of the church's pocket will be spent, neither. He will stay in my home, and it will be a joyous celebration—hallelujah!"

After three days spent in his office mulling it all over, Reverend Blue had rejected the idea. There would be no outsiders coming between the congregation and one of God's holiest unions.

"Adam and Eve had no officiant, nor the daughters of Lot after fleeing the destruction of Sodom." Blue said it in that voice that brokered no argument. Not quite a holy command, but deep enough and cold enough that Donnie Ray had averted his eyes and not mentioned his cousin again.

He never once asked for Dallas' opinion. Why would he, when it was not needed? Dallas had nothing to say about it anyway. The ceremony was all based in what Blue wanted—what he felt was necessary. If standing before God and declaring Dallas his husband proper was what it took to cleanse his spirit of depravity then so be it. Dallas could hardly look at him without picturing how flushed his face had been back at the parish, or without remembering how eagerly his hot tongue had shoved its way into Dallas' mouth.

With that in mind, it was no small wonder that Blue did not want another pastor to be present. That man would be able to see right through him. So-And-So from Birmingham would take one look at Blue and see his shame-stained soul, but the congregation could not know.

"Dallas." Blue's voice pulled him from his thoughts.

"Hm?" Dallas glanced up.

Blue leaned over the side of the table where Dallas was sitting and pushed a piece of yellow notebook paper across the surface.

"Pulled pork barbecue for the reception, or cold finger sandwiches?" he asked. "Sister Marge Elsie wants to know."

Dallas crinkled his nose. "I don't think it makes a difference," he said. "Either option is near guaranteed to confine me to the toilet."

Blue's smile thinned. "I think barbecue." He swept the paper back up. "That is always popular with our older folks." He marked something down in pen. "Carol from the ladies' sewing circle says that they will have your suit finished sometime this afternoon for you to try on."

Dallas straightened in his wheelchair and a flash of anger warmed his face.

"I can tailor my own clothes," he said. "I have been for two years."

"Yes," Blue said dismissively, "but you do not have to now, so you won't."

"The only thing I have to do is marry you, apparently," Dallas snipped back. Even as he spoke, regret reeled back the rest of his words. He bit the inside of his cheek and watched Blue's expression shift from mild to stormy grey.

"It is God's will," Blue spat out each syllable as if Dallas had not heard it a hundred times over already. "It is not our place to question the Almighty!"

"I have not questioned Him," Dallas said. He softened his voice just enough to make it clear he was not challenging the reverend. "I have had my wonderings, I cannot lie, but in the end I will do as God has ordained."

"Dallas." Reverend Blue took one of Dallas' hands and clasped it between both of his own. "Even the seed of a doubt can become embedded in our minds. It only needs a drop of water to take root. Before you know it, doubt is an oak tree, and you are always living in its shadow. You need to take that seed and pluck it out. Pluck it out and throw it to the wayside. Do you understand me?"

Dallas nodded. "I understand," he said. He looked down at Blue's hands. The reverend had nails like polished glass and fingers as cold as steel.

"We don't have much," Blue continued. "But we will stand before the Lord and make a promise to each other, to live our lives for Him and obey without question. As Abraham would have sacrificed his son Isaac, we must be willing to give everything to Him."

Dallas looked up. "Would you sacrifice me?" he asked, keeping his tone light as he pulled his hand out of Blue's grip. "Would you lay me out on a shabby altar and drive a stone knife through my heart?"

"If the Lord commanded it," Blue said grimly.

"I will bear that in mind," Dallas said.

There was not a trace of doubt in his mind over that, at least. He knew that Blue meant every word.

The ceremony took place beneath the heavily burdened boughs of peach trees. The pale pink fruits hung low, sumptuous and suggestive with tight, swollen sides and deep, fuzzy clefts. Their dark leaves were still slick with lingering morning dew, and Dallas envied every engorged, glistening drop that seemed to mock his own pent-up state.

He wanted to feel nothing. And yet, his attention was inescapably drawn to everything in that moment. His suit was too itchy and too tight. It hugged all the wrong places. Whoever had been in charge of taking it in had paid special attention to his waist and just underneath his bust. He had sewn the sides of his binder together to the point where it was almost impossible to breathe in, and it was still not enough to make up for the bad tailoring. It was hot, too. He was dripping sweat. His curls stuck behind his ears and against the nape of his neck. And even with Brother Leon playing soft notes on his six-string banjo to take the edge off the silence, Dallas could hear everything that went on around him. He heard heels shuffling in the grass. He heard wads of gum being swatted between gnashing teeth and flapping gums. He heard whispers and titters, muffled coughs and stifled yawns. Behind every attentive gaze he could see the glazed eyes of boredom. Without a visiting pastor to lead the ceremony, it was just Blue and Dallas with their hands locked together—standing in a grove and praying while the sun rose and dragged the heat behind it. Every shift and shuffle drove him crazy. Every murmur made him feel like he was going to crawl out of his skin. He did not know what he wanted, except to be anywhere else.

If Blue was bothered, it did not show. He wore his devout concentration about as handsomely as his blood-red suit. Brassy blond hair, sharp blue eyes, and yards of crimson fabric—he resembled the morning sky, a piece of dawn that had been carved out and flung down to earth like the rotten part of a peach. With his eyes turned towards heaven, a thread of light shot down his jaw, edging him in gold like a portrait of a saint.

It bought to Dallas' mind an image of Saint Sebastian, full of arrows. He was not sure why.

Finally, Reverend Blue lowered his head. Somewhere during the motion, he transformed. No longer a saint or an archangel, he looked entirely human. Not Reverend Blue, or even just Blue, but Blessing Easton with a boyish smile like a young man on his wedding day. The transformation only lasted as long as it took Dallas to blink. By the time Blue reached out to take his hand, he seemed entirely himself again. The grin had vanished and there was only his firm, set mouth again. The shape his narrow lips had warped into could hardly be counted as a smile, despite its upward curve.

"Dallas Hackett." Blue caressed Dallas' hand in his. "Today we are joined spiritually in holy matrimony. Created in the likeness of our savior..."

He continued to speak, but Dallas was no longer listening. Blue's words could not drown out the chewing, the smacking, the grinding of the congregation.

Big, round dewdrops rolled down the sides of taut, herculean fruits.

Sweat started to bead on Blue's upper lip.

Dallas clenched his thighs together.

"Amen," Blue said. He squeezed Dallas' fingers.

"Amen," Dallas rasped out, even though he had not processed the rest of the reverend's words.

Blue pulled a ring from out of nowhere. It was a simple gold band, slightly tarnished and a little bent. Yet, it fit Dallas' ring finger almost perfectly. Blue raised Dallas' hand to his mouth and kissed the ring's place, dragging his lips slightly along the metal.

Dallas flicked his tongue over his bottom lip and smiled even though he was not sure if he was supposed to.

The congregation hollered so apparently, that was right.

CHAPTER NINE

HIS BANNER OVER ME
IS LOVE

Even though it was his second time inside the parish, Dallas felt no more in control than he had on his first visit. If anything, the second time around was worse because he could not leave.

'Not entirely true', he corrected his own thoughts. He could walk away, theoretically—but it was expected that he would not. Besides, where would he go? Back to his grandfather's house? That belonged to Blue now, too. Blue was the long shadow creeping over Wicker and the earth shrank everywhere he touched. Wicker had started out small, and the reverend's world was even smaller. He took what he saw and he pressed it together, forming it in the shape of the Church of New Lazarus. And whatever did not fit...

A heavy thump jolted Dallas back to the moment. He placed his hand against the bolo tie at his throat—a modest silver cross with a probably-fake red jewel in the center. He loosened the tie in order to excuse the action.

Blue rested his hand on top of the bible he had dropped onto his end table and closed his eyes. His mouth moved, but no sound came out. When he opened his eyes, he turned towards Dallas without a single trace of a readable expression on his face.

"I dreamt of you last night," Blue said. When he spoke, he flicked his gaze up and down, analyzing the young man in front of him while loosening his own bolo.

"Did you?" Dallas asked. He slid the leather lace out the side of his collar and let the whole tie crumple in his lap. He set his hands against the wheels of his chair, but he did not move any closer to his new husband. "What was this dream like?"

"I dreamt that you were afraid," Blue told him. "I know that it was God telling me to be gentle with you on our first night." He tilted his head. "You do not need to be afraid of me."

Dallas smiled bitterly. "I am not," he said. He was damned if he was a liar, but he did not care. "I think you forget that we have been here before."

Blue glanced over at the bedroom door, as if turning the memory over in his head. "We have been there." He turned his eyes to the bed. "But not here."

Dallas gripped his wheels a little tighter. It did not matter that his stomach quivered and that he felt like he was going to throw up. He was simply unwilling to play the role of blushing virgin on his wedding night. He realized that he didn't care, either, if that was how Blue liked it. It was a strange dichotomy deep in his brain where he could not seem to decide exactly how he felt about the reverend. Blue frightened him, sure, and if he wanted to—he could command Dallas to do anything with that voice. But then, Dallas had been through the death of his grandfather, the loss of his home, and made a deal with the devil all in the span of a week. He had nothing to else to lose, not even his soul.

It was liberating in the sense that his flesh could do no worse. It was equally terrifying for the same reason.

"Well." Dallas' voice sounded wobbly, and he cleared his throat to strengthen it. "That's hardly my fault, is it?" He leaned back in his chair and paused to take a deep breath.

"Do you need help?" Blue asked. He took a step forward. "I can bring you over to the bed."

"I can do it," Dallas said, "I just need a minute." He looked down. The tops of his white shoes were covered in mud from walking back and forth through the grove. "If you could help me with my shoes, I would appreciate that. I don't know how far down I can bend."

Reverend Blue nodded. He closed the distance between them and then sank down to one knee, slipping his hand underneath Dallas' shoe to cup his heel and then slide it off. He did not even need to unlace them.

He set one shoe to the side before starting on the other. Once they were both off, he pinched the top of Dallas' black sock and began to roll it down his calf. A muscle flexed in

Blue's throat as he swallowed, and his breath seemed to hitch as he set one bare foot down and took the other socked one in his hands.

Dallas watched him curiously. He flexed his bare toes, turning over a dozen possibilities in his mind while watching Blue slide the sock down his skin with almost reverent care. Once it was off, Blue lingered over his foot— pushing his thumb into Dallas' arch and sliding it up towards the pad underneath his toes. Dallas bit his lip against a groan of pleasure that nearly escaped and he leaned back further in his wheelchair, raking his nails over the plush leather arms.

Dallas brought his other bare foot up and pressed his toes down against Blue's shoulder. Blue glanced up at him, and in that split moment, something on his face changed. It piqued Dallas' curiosity to see it—something quietly desperate that made Blue's eyes light up while his cheeks came alive with a heated flush. His lips parted, slightly, and a soft gasp eked out in a tightly controlled burst of air.

It was a window of opportunity, and Dallas could not let it pass. He pulled his bare toes down Blue's shoulder, dragging on his suit jacket lightly, before trailing them back up and tapping Blue's cheek playfully. The reverend looked up through thick, bronze lashes and took hold of Dallas' foot. He massaged the sole again, using both hands to work his fingers up and down the slender sides. Dallas pressed his toes against Blue's lips, dragging the bottom one down, and Blue's tongue came out to slide over the very tips. He ran his hand up Dallis' leg while doing so, pushing his red trousers up to the knee and exposing the length of the young man's creamy freckled calf. Blue kneaded his fingers into the malleable flesh, eliciting a deep groan that Dallas could not control from his lips. Dallas' entire body shivered and he gripped the arms of his wheelchair, halfway afraid that if he leaned too far back then the whole thing might tip over. Blue pressed in closer, placing his greedy lips against Dallas' calf and sucking while his free hand continued to knead his arch. Dallas' toes curled inward and his calf muscles tensed as a thread of pleasure ran the length of his body and twinged in his throat, making his voice breathy as he spoke.

"Take off your shirt," Dallas said. It was a command, not a request. He waited to see what Blue would do—if there was a consequence for being so brazen, or if he had correctly weighed and measured his new husband's response.

The pause lasted only a moment. Blue lowered Dallas' foot carefully and then rocked back to rest against his heels. He raised his chin high and those long, flashy fingers went to work. He stripped off his suit jacket in one motion and tossed it aside. Then he started in on his bolo tie, unclipping the back and sliding it down the leather laces that wrapped underneath his sharply folded collar. The tie landed against the carpet with a dull thud, and then came his shirt. The buttons came apart easily, revealing the full expanse of his tanned chest and the spread of downy gold chair that plunged down between the separation of his sculpted pectorals. A dainty gold chain bearing a small gold cross no bigger than a thumbnail dangled there, resting just below the hollow of his throat.

Moving his gaze a little lower, Dallas caught a peek of black. But it was not until Blue had peeled his shirt away entirely that the full picture was revealed. Thin, dark scars wound their way around his chest—starting at the separation and ending underneath his arms in pinched, knotted tissue. Paler puncture scars like stitch-holes dotted the wine-red line, although the majority of it was covered by the tattoo of a black, bloody-headed vulture with its tattered wings outstretched across Blue's ribcage.

The downy blond hair disappeared into the bird and re-emerged on the other side, plunging past his sharp hips and disappearing down the line of his trousers.

Dallas swallowed hard and set his hand against his own chest, feeling the need to reassure himself that his heart was still beating.

"I did not know," Dallas said carefully, "that God permitted such modifications."

Blue gave him a wounded look, another blindsiding human expression. True vulnerability from an impenetrable fortress of a man.

"I thought you of all people might understand," Blue said.

"I meant," Dallas prodded the center of his chest with his toes, "the tattoo."

"Oh." Blue's shoulders sagged as a breath escaped his lips. "Yes. Well." He sat up straight on his knees, keeping his hands resting in his lap with the palms turned upward, the picture of poise. "Are you telling me that you don't have any?"

Dallas could not help the smile that spread across his face. "No, I don't," he said. He dragged his toes down Blue's chest. "Although, are you going to take my word for it?"

Blue caught his ankle and pulled himself closer. The wheelchair moved and Dallas gasped, but Blue grabbed the brake and pulled it so that it was clutched up against the wheel.

"I am not going to let you go anywhere," Blue said. He pushed Dallas' trouser leg up high over his knee and kissed it, stroking his calf and kneading with his strong fingers.

"Undress me," Dallas breathed. Blue did as he was told. He moved up Dallas' body and began to work his jacket down his shoulders. Dallas twisted impatiently. He squirmed out of the arms and flung the jacket aside as fast as he could. Suddenly, it was too hot. It was hot, and it itched, and he wanted to be naked. Naked and vulnerable just like Blue. Two people, face-to-face, with nothing between them except the light of the Holy Spirit.

Dallas' buttons were all too eager to spring apart for Blue's fingers. The reverend made short work of Dallas' white dress shirt, and then the hand-sewn binder quickly followed. It was a pain to wrench off, even with Blue to pull it up over his head. Dallas almost gave up. He nearly screamed at Blue to just cut it off, but then the binder slid off his arms and joined the rest of the clothes on the floor.

Dallas' breasts tumbled free, soft and heavy with creamy erect nipples jutting out from the sudden rush of cold. Blue placed his hands on them immediately, gazing down as if he was cradling a priceless treasure. Dallas lowered his head and placed his hands on either side of Blue's face until the reverend looked up and their noses scraped together.

"I am still wearing pants," Dallas whispered. Their lips were so close that he could feel every one of Blue's trembling breaths. "And so are you."

Blue remedied that quickly. He pressed his mouth against each of Dallas' breasts in turn, kissing them, flicking his tongue over the nipples and pinching them between his fingers before making his descent. He kissed all the way down Dallas' chest and over his soft stomach, working his pants down his hips at the same time. He dragged everything with him—trousers, underwear, and all. Blue tossed it aside and it disappeared from the corners of Dallas' vision. Out of sight, out of mind. Now Dallas was thoroughly naked, and still seated in his wheelchair. He gazed down at Blue who kept himself occupied by sucking on the inside of Dallas' thighs. The reverend raised one of Dallas' legs until it was perched on his shoulder and let it rest there, using the newfound leverage to better access what he was searching for. The reverend's tongue danced up Dallas' skin, moving over his glazed inner thigh, already slick with his anticipation. Dallas threw his head back and moaned, unable to resist digging his fingers into Blue's golden hair and pushing his head down.

Blue took the silent command. He buried his head between Dallas' thighs, wrapping his arms up underneath him to hold him by the hips. Dallas wrapped both his legs around Blue's shoulders and dug his heels into the reverend's back. Blue's tongue circled his entrance, hot and wet, prodding curiously before slipping up and down, as if trying to decide the best approach. Dallas moaned, unable to control the sounds he made. Blue's tongue dove deeper, plunging into him, filling him up and then pulling back. Dallas cried out, and Blue thrust his tongue inside again. When he pulled it out the second time, he flattened it and dragged it all the way up towards Dallas' swollen, hot clit. Blue's fingers intervened, stroking the entrance that the reverend's tongue had abandoned. They slid inside, just the tips at first, two at a time. The reverend twisted and thrust with his fingers, working them back and forth until he was two knuckles deep. All the while his tongue continued its work, circling Dallas' clit and drawing it into his mouth, sucking and licking—gorging himself like a man starving. With each pull of his greedy mouth Dallas cried out again. His legs trembled and his back arched, which only caused him to dig his heels deeper between Blue's shoulders. Blue pressed his face against Dallas' entrance until his nose was buried in his flesh and he kept sucking, pushing his fingers in as deep as they could go and using his whole hand to make hard, deep thrusts.

Dallas could not take it. He was overwhelmed—dizzy with pleasure. The world was spinning and not even his grip on his wheelchair was enough to let him feel grounded. The pleasure expanded in his belly, filling him with warmth and making everything feel tighter than a spring. He did not know how long Blue was down there, and he was slightly self-conscious about taking too long to allow himself to orgasm. But then, he had never had another person give him an orgasm before. Was it that much different than giving one to yourself?

The pleasure erupted without warning. Dallas screamed and gripped Blue's hair so tightly that the reverend growled against his cunt. Dallas rode his face, holding him down and squeezing out every last bit of ecstasy that he could. When Blue finally emerged, his face was shiny and drenched by Dallas' orgasm. An apostle's fiery baptism, and Dallas felt higher than Christ.

"Did I do good?" Blue asked. He kept staring at Dallas' cunt, as if enamored by the glory of his own work.

"You did beautifully." Dallas dragged himself up into a sitting position even though he was out of breath. He pulled his thighs together—how hot and wet they were, how they ached. "Do you want me to try it with you?" He had never gone down on anyone before, but it felt like a sin not to return the favor when he had been so thoroughly ravaged.

"I," Blue cleared his throat and glanced towards the bed. "I have a different—request."

"Sure." Dallas held out his hand and Blue stood up. The reverend took his hand and helped him out of the chair. On weak and trembling knees, Dallas made his way to the bed and oozed onto the side. He rolled over onto his back and spread his legs again, unable to resist touching himself and the mess that Blue had made.

Blue unbuttoned his own trousers and slid his hand down the front. He pulled out a lump of skin-toned silicone and set it down on the bedside table. Dallas rolled his head over and spared the item a glance. It was shaped like a soft penis—beautifully crafted with blue veins and a dark pink head. He smiled at the sight for no reason other than he was giddy, and his head was still swimming.

Blue finished undressing and then reached into the beside table's drawer. He withdrew a bottle of lube and set it down on top, and then he pulled out a mess of supple leather straps and a bright red dildo that was as thick as a fist.

Dallas' eyes widened and he sat up. Blue settled onto the bed and held up the strap-on, all traces of embarrassment having fled his handsome face.

"It's, um." Dallas licked his lips. "It is a little bit big."

"I have used it on myself before," Blue said, keeping his gaze steady. "But now I want you to use it on me. I call it St. Michael."

Dallas took hold of the dildo and set it down to unravel the straps. The leather was very high quality and painted with gold—a detail he had not noticed before.

"I will try," Dallas said. "I have never done it before."

"All I ask is that you try," Blue said.

Dallas stared at the dildo for a little longer and then shrugged.

"Turn around," he said.

Blue looked away. Dallas slid off the side of the bed and pulled the straps up over his hips. He tightened the buckles until everything was snug and then he pushed the dildo through the ring in the center. He swiveled his hips and grabbed the dildo to bounce it a bit, feeling a little silly but wanting to make sure it wouldn't fly off. He liked the way it felt, dangling from between his legs. He felt like a man, but in a way that could only be bought.

Dallas made his way back onto the bed and grabbed the lube as he went. Blue slid into a downward position immediately, grabbing onto a pillow and stuffing it underneath his arms to give himself some support. He put his ass in the air and spread his legs, digging his knees into the bed and turning his face to the side.

Dallas did not know how much lube to use. The dildo was enormous, in his opinion, so he opted for more on the side of caution. He dribbled the lube down Blue's ass cheeks and covered both his entrances, using his hand to spread it around until everything was coated and glistening. Blue jumped at the first contact, but settled down almost immediately. There was excess on Dallas' hands, so he slid it up and down his red cock before placing his hands against Blue's hips and leaning over.

"Which one?" he asked. He thrust his hips and teased Blue with the tip while he asked.

"In my ass," Blue said. His face was already flushed. Dallas smiled and pulled his hips back, grabbing the dildo by its base and moving it up so that it was pressed up against the reverend's second hole.

The tight ring of muscle did not want to give way, but Dallas coaxed it with his fingers, pushing the tips through until Blue had relaxed enough for him to try with the dildo. He pushed the head inside first, moving slowly, listening to every one of Blue's moans for any change that might indicate pain. Dallas worked his way inside until his hips were pressed against Blue's ass. Then he started to rock back and forth, working and thrusting the dildo from every angle. He started slowly at first then built up speed, pushing himself up onto his knees so that he could lean over Blue's back and hold onto his hips as he thrust.

Blue was lost in his own pleasure, moaning and gasping. He writhed on Dallas' red cock, pushing himself down to the hilt, digging his fingers into his bed and pulling up fistfuls of his blanket in his white knuckles. He ground his teeth and muttered a litany of prayers, at some point moving into a language that Dallas did not recognize—like he was speaking in tongues. He spread his legs as wide as they could go and pushed his head down until Dallas thought his neck was going to break. Blue shoved one hand underneath himself, touching his own cunt, spreading it wider with his fingers and stroking his own clit.

"Good?" Dallas gasped.

"Good!" Blue groaned. "More, yes, yes, just like that—God, God, fuck me!"

Dallas thrust faster, driving himself as hard and as deep as he could each time. Blue's prayers became even louder, every desperate word stumbling off his tongue, clumsy and begging. The rush that Dallas felt with his husband pinned underneath his hips was better than any orgasm. He felt like he could cum again just like that, with the strap-on rubbing against him, and Blue writhing, pleading for his mercy.

"God, God, God—" Blue stammered. His whole body shook, breaking out into a feverish sweat that trickled down his spine.

"Dallas," Dallas hissed. He grabbed Blue's ass and squeezed it as he thrust. "In bed, I am Elohim."

"Elohim!" Blue cried. "I need, I will—"

"You will not," Dallas said. "Not without asking."

"Please!" Blue choked.

"In tongues," Dallas hissed.

Blue's tongue launched into a string of words that did not make any sense strung together. The words themselves did not matter, anyway. Dallas was far more satisfied by the action. He leaned over far enough to press his hand against Blue's head, gripping his hair once again and driving his face down into the bed as he fucked him.

"Good boy," Dallas said. "Good. Beautiful. Yes. All right. You can release for me, yes, you've earned it. So good. Wonderful. Beautiful!"

Blue's body quivered and he rocked forward, releasing onto his fingers and clenching down around the dildo. He held himself there for a moment, unable to speak. The only sound he could make was a strangled moan that finally wrenched itself free as he slid off the dildo and collapsed into the bedsheets.

The dildo rested searing-hot and heavy against Dallas' thigh. He did not want to take it off. He fell onto his back and rolled over onto his side, resting his hand against Blue's shoulder. Blue rolled over until his back was pressed against Dallas' chest. His tanned skin was flushed red, and the beads of sweat rolling down his forehead soaked his hair as well.

Dallas kissed Blue's shoulder, rubbing his upper arm at the same time.

"Did I do good?" Dallas asked, echoing Blue's earlier words.

"Amazing," Blue let out the words on a ragged, grateful breath. "Absolutely divine."

CHAPTER TEN

BE THOU MY VISION

When Dallas dreamt of his grandfather's house, it groaned, trembling as though it rested on the back of a massive beast's tongue. The wooden floors and nicotine-stained walls croaked out that low, unholy sound while warping and swaying underneath his feet. He was dizzy, and his brain felt swollen—as though it had soaked up a gallon of water like a sponge and was now just slamming into the front and back of his skull whenever he stumbled. He knew that he was dreaming, but he could not make himself stand up properly. His knees shook too much, and every time he regained his balance, it was lost again when the floor dipped or rolled.

Grainy vinyl popping over the sound of a crooning quartet drifted through the house where he was not alone, but he knew in his gut that his grandfather wasn't there, either. How could he be? He was dead. Even in the dream, Dallas knew that.

Something crashed at the top of the staircase and Dallas gasped. His tongue was too big for his mouth and the surprised breath choked him. He shoved his swollen tongue between his teeth to let it sit, as if the edges of his incisors could prevent it from puffing up any further. Excess saliva ran from the hanging cavity of his mouth. Between that and his swimming head, he wondered if he was having a stroke or a seizure in his sleep. He was just lucid enough to know that he was dreaming, but not enough to wake himself up.

Dallas found himself facing the staircase where the top three steps were eclipsed by a deep shadow. He collapsed to his knees and his teeth pierced through his tongue. He yelped in pain, but he could not pry his jaw open without also digging out his teeth. He tried using both hands, but his nails sank into his gums like they were made of putty, and beyond the throbbing pain he tasted copper.

He raised his head again with his fingers still pushed through the corners of his cheeks, hooked into the slimy insides. The top half of his tongue dangled over his bottom lip, hanging on by just a thread, it felt like. The house groaned again—the sound a more mournful, cetacean wail than before.

Underneath the overwhelming taste of blood, smoke tickled the back of Dallas' throat. He pulled his fingers out of his mouth and blood gushed from the sides of his cheeks like water. Suddenly, the pressure in his cheeks was relieved and the tension in his jaw loosened enough for him to open his mouth again. With a soft 'click' his tongue tumbled out of his mouth and fell to the ground—a lump of pale, pink flesh covered in dirt. Two of his teeth were still embedded in the sides, dull ivory and half-eaten by cavities.

The smoke was pouring from the top of the stairs. Dallas used his elbows and his knees to push himself along the floor, determined to inch closer and see where the smoke was coming from. He got as far as the bottom step and reached out to grab onto its lip. His fingertips smeared blood along the wood, where there were deep scars with bits of nail embedded in the pale runs.

Like someone had been trying to hold onto the steps as they were dragged all the way up. The scars disappeared into the shadow.

A white shoe appeared near the top of the stairs. It was immediately swallowed by a swirl of bright yellow silk as its twin descended to join its side. Dallas raised his head a little higher, craning his neck until it ached to see as far up as he could. His gaze slid over yards of canary-colored silk draped over a hoop skirt and padded by rustling crinoline that grated against his eardrums like squirming maggots. The neckline plunged and ended in a gleaming topaz set in a silver brooch. The topaz felt like an eye somehow, dead and yellow, gazing down at him apathetically from on high.

Another cloud of pale smoke appeared, curling over flushed bare shoulders with an exquisitely placed mole right against the collarbone. Dallas recognized the devil, now, even with their long brown hair curled into ringlets and spray of baby's breath flowers nestled close to their ear. They looked down at Dallas and smiled, peeling back their lusciously formed lips to bare sharp, monstrous teeth. They opened their mouth and their throat convulsed. Their prominent larynx bobbed and their skin bubbled as if there was something inside of them pressing against their throat, fighting to claw its way out.

The devil's whole body convulsed. They pressed their hands against their corseted stomach and lurched forward. Their mouth continued to stretch until the corners split, and blood raced down along the sides of their chin to collect underneath.

Then, from their mouth, Dallas caught sight of a pointed, reptilian face. 'Like a cobra.' He just knew that was what it was. It slithered its way out, as yellow as bile with black speckles along its sides. Dallas could not help but think that it looked like a rotten banana. The snake slid out of the devil's mouth, heavy and thick, weaving its taut body through the air as if swaying to an invisible song.

Then, the snake stopped. Its back end was still sliding out of the devil's mouth, miles and miles of never-ending yellow coils. The snake was inches from his face, and its black tongue flickered, tickling Dallas' nose. Then, the snake reared back. It opened its mouth and flared its hood, and Dallas tried to scream. No sound came out, and he wondered if it was because his tongue was on the ground. Could he no longer scream, without his tongue?

allas opened his eyes. He was stuck on his side with his arm trapped underneath him. He tried to speak, but his jaw felt locked. He tried to push out a sound, any sound, but all he managed was a panicked groan that circled around the top of his throat.

Was he dead?

He tried not to panic. Dallas closed his eyes and tried to circulate first one, then two steady breaths. His arm tingled, but he still could not move his fingers. He whimpered again, and this time the sound pushed itself out between his lips. Although there were still no words, just a dumb, weeping cry like a trapped animal.

"Dallas?" Blue's voice, thick with sleep, came from the other side of the bed. Blue touched his shoulder and pulled him back. The movement was just enough of a jolt to bring him fully back and Dallas gasped, twitching at first, but then raising his arm in a swift and sudden movement that sent his hand crashing into Blue's jaw.

"I'm sorry!" Dallas gasped. He was drenched in sweat. The bedsheets were stuck against his legs and he peeled them back, kicking them off even though his entire body still felt like it was made of lead. Pain throbbed in his temple like an iron nail had been lodged in the bone, but he was grateful to feel it. Pain meant that he was alive.

"I've had worse," Blue said dismissively. "What were you dreaming?"

It took Dallas a moment to collect his thoughts. He found himself laying back against a thick pillow, staring up into Blue's cold cornflower eyes, the reverend's expression as flat as pressed flowers.

"I—" Dallas did not know how to respond. He raised his still-tingling hand to rub his face, trying to sort out the disturbing imagery of his nightmare before it all disappeared. "It was the devil." Dallas finally managed to push the words out. "The devil came to me as a yellow serpent."

"The color of betrayal," Blue said without a second's hesitation. "And a snake. A traitor in our midst."

"Yes," Dallas told him. He sat up a bit against the pillow and turned further into Blue's arms. "The seeds of discontent that have been sown will yield a baneful crop." He was not quite sure what he was trying to say. The words just rolled off his tongue and Blue seemed to agree with them, so he kept going. "It may be that someone in the congregation is unhappy with our union, and in doubting God, they have let the devil in."

Blue nodded along to every word, swallowing the babbling narrative that was being fed to him by Dallas' dream-dulled wits and his terror of discovery. After all, if Blue discovered that he had been consorting with the devil—Dallas remembered that feeling of being struck over the head, unable to stand or speak, and it made him shiver. He did not want to die in Blue's bed.

And he did not doubt, for one minute, that the reverend would strike him down.

"It is the Holy Spirit," Blue finally said. "It is the Holy Spirit speaking through you to give us a message. A warning. We need a revival."

"Yes," Dallas agreed. He pressed his hand against Blue's naked chest and kissed the reverend's throat. "A revival."

"Tomorrow, I will announce it to the congregation," Blue said. "A week-long revival where we can call the sinners to repent. And if the devil darkens our doorstep we will cast him out and any who gives him their alliance."

"The devil will not live here," Dallas said. He stroked his finger over Blue's larynx and kissed his jaw. "Not in Wicker."

"Not in Wicker, not in this church." Blue agreed. Dallas just wanted to drift back to sleep, but Blue was more awake now than before, and all fired up. If he had been clothed, Dallas could see him dashing down to the pulpit to spit the fiery sermon that was clearly percolating.

"But tomorrow," Dallas said. He was too comfortable, and he did not want Blue to get up. "Tomorrow is for revival. Tonight is for sleep. Don't let the devil drive you from your marital bed."

Blue paused like he was considering it all, and then he nodded. "Right." He wrapped his arms around Dallas and squeezed. "But we need to pray, before we sleep again. We need to thank God that He brought us this warning. We need to thank Him for choosing you as a vessel of the Holy Spirit."

Dallas held back and sigh and nodded. Blue placed a hand against his forehead and grasped it tight, clenching as hard as he could while digging his fingers into the sides of Dallas' aching temples as he began to pray and give thanks.

CHAPTER ELEVEN

WE GATHER TOGETHER

The white revival tent had more peaks than a mountain range and covered half an acre on its own. It stood as tall as the church trailer itself and had no entrances or windows, save for the very front. Sunday morning's sermon had called for a revival of 'Old Testament proportions' and by noon, volunteers were pulling the poles and folded canvas out from church storage. The ladies passed around a meal roster where they each wrote down the contributions they would bring. Even the children were encouraged to help by stomping on the heads of tent stakes until they were driven 'too deep in the dirt for the devil to rip out'.

It had been a long time since Wicker had seen a tent revival. Dallas had a faint memory of one from a few years back, before Blue ever entered the picture. Every good Christian loved the opportunity to reignite their fire for the Lord while stomping on the devil's tail—or however Blue had phrased it. He had neglected to tell them the real reason for it all, that he suspected sedition.

And now Dallas was Pastor Dallas, although the honorific was the only thing that had changed about his relationship with the congregation. It was not accompanied by any new shows of respect or deference. If anything, their judgment was more palpable. Every eye that lingered over him seemed too knowledgeable of exactly what had occurred between him and the reverend. Dirty and exposed, that was how they saw him. Their silent accusations expressed an impossible paradox. He would have been a whore for occupying the reverend's bed before marriage, but he bore the proverbial scarlet letter anyway because in their collective opinion, he had turned the head of a powerful prophet. It was sin and seduction. In their eyes, Dallas was the yellow serpent and the betrayer. And if they considered him anything worse, he no longer caught wind of it. They wired their jaws shut around him. He had lost even the privilege of an eavesdropper.

The tent was erected by supper time, and the menfolk brought out folding chairs and a big metal fan to set up near the makeshift pulpit. By Blue's specifications, they had laid down a makeshift stage of two thick pieces of plywood and a rubber mat. He stomped down a few times to test its sturdiness, and the tent was filled with the righteous striking of his heel.

Dallas hovered near the tent entrance while Blue tested out the sound equipment. The smell of hot dogs boiling in a vat of baked beans from the reception trailer's kitchen made him nauseous, and knowing that there would be hours more before he could crawl into bed was depressing. The Alabama summer heat sent boulders of sweat trickling down the back of his shirt. His high collar was soaked and his red curls stuck to his neck and behind his ears in clumps. The heat did not seem to affect Blue in the same way. It only flushed his cheeks and made his eyes brighter. It made him more alive, like a steaming kettle sounding the alarm over the fires of Hell.

One of the tent flaps crinkled and a body stepped into Dallas' peripheral vision. A few steps more into the tent and he recognized the person as Brother Rory—a big man with wide shoulders who was old enough to be Dallas' father. He had both hands wrapped around the thick, scarred handle of a shovel, and on the end of it was a lump of fur covered in pine needles.

"Reverend!" Brother Rory called out. Dallas felt an itch of annoyance that he had not been addressed as well, but he let that go. He gripped the rims of his wheels and propelled himself closer, very pointedly putting himself into the bigger man's path.

"Is there something that you need, Brother Rory?" Dallas asked. The older man cut him an exasperated look.

"I need to show this to the reverend -" he held up his shovel and shook it a bit - "what my wife found in the barn when she was going to feed the goats."

"The reverend is busy," Dallas said. "He is preparing for tonight's revival. You are free to show me, or I can—"

Before he could finish, a hand landed on his shoulder and squeezed, cutting off his words mid-air. Blue's voice slipped its way into the conversation, easy and smooth, gliding right over the broken pause.

"Good evening, Brother Rory," Reverend Blue said. "Is there something that I can help you with?" He kept his hand on Dallas' shoulder as he spoke, the weight of his Rolex watch bearing down onto the younger man's trapezius.

"This." Rory lifted his shovel again. "You might want to have a look, reverend. We found this in our barn. Missus figured it was just another kitten that died because it lost its mama. We get them all the time. But look..." Rory tipped his shovel's point towards the ground and the furry lump slid off the metal. It hit the grass with a soft thud, Dallas leaned over to get a better look.

"Black cat." Brother Rory wiped his forehead. "With two heads." He prodded the lump with his foot hard enough to make the stiff limbs uncurl, and the head of the thing bowed back enough for Dallas to get a real good look if he squinted. It did not properly have two heads. It was more like two faces stuck onto the same form. There were two noses and two mouths, with two sets of tiny white fangs peeking out from the sides. There were two sets of eyes, although they were closed. Four perfect little crescent moons ruling over a revolting night sky. There were only two ears, though. Two ears, four eyes. One neck.

Dallas' stomach roiled. Over his shoulder, he heard Blue take in a sharp breath.

"The adversary prowls around like a roaring lion, seeking someone to devour." Blue stamped his heel against the ground. "Oh, Brother, Satan is in our midst. He walks among us today. We must cast him out today!"

Dallas tried not to roll his eyes. He dragged his nails up and down the arms of his wheelchair, unable to stop staring at the dead kitten.

"Blue," he said quietly, "save some of that for your sermon."

He looked up as soon as the words left his mouth. Brother Rory stared at him, eyes almost bugging out of his head. It was as good as a public admonishment. A few days ago, Dallas would have never dared. He expected his heart to drop into his stomach or to bang against his ribs until it burst, but instead, he was overtaken by a sense of calm. Whether or not he had a right to be, he was sure of himself in that moment.

The uncomfortable pause lasted only for a breath. Blue squeezed Dallas' shoulder again, more acknowledgment than ownership.

"You're right," he said. "No sense in wasting the Lord's fire." He jabbed a condemning finger at the dead cat. "Take that out into the woods and burn it. Then come back, brother, and we will pray for you. We will pray for you and your wife tonight that the devil releases his hold on you."

"Thank you, Reverend." Brother Rory sounded a little choked up as he scooped the cat back up with his shovel. "Missus and I won't be more than an hour."

lue was born for open-air preaching. Some pastors, once you yanked them down from the comfort of their pulpits, were lost when the surroundings became bigger than they were, and their voices were amplified by stacked speakers. Not Reverend Blue. The revival tent was not big enough for him. He jumped up and down, stamping his feet and throwing his fists into the air. He preached until he was red in the face and his blond hair was drenched in sweat. His cornflower eyes were shiny and bright, and spit flew from his white teeth as he cursed the devil into his microphone. He had the congregation wailing in their seats, throwing themselves to the ground and babbling in tongues. He had their arms raised towards the heavens, shaking with hands flapping wildly back and forth as tears streamed down their cheeks. The Holy Spirit of Revival was thick in the air, and even with the flaps at the tent's entrance tied back, it still felt like soup. It still smelled like department store catalog perfume and dirt. The discordant notes from the church keyboard still sounded like a yowling mountain cat.

Blue was in the thick of it all. He stood in front of the pulpit with his right hand raised towards Heaven and his left clutching the microphone to his chest. Members of the congregation swarmed around him like flies to honey, stuck to his side on their hands and knees, grabbing onto whatever pieces of him they could whether it was an arm or his jacket hem. They loved him. Oh, they loved him. He was their salvation. He was their voice from God. He would cast the devil from their midst and save the little town of Wicker. He was their redeemer. Their savior. He lay his hands on them, and they wailed until their voices were lost.

Dallas watched from behind the pulpit. He sat with his hands crossed over Blue's bible that rested in his lap. It was old, heavy leather with gilded pages and so large that Dallas had to pick it up with both hands. He didn't know how Blue threw it around like it was nothing, smacking it against the pulpit and thrusting it into people's faces. Dallas' eyes scanned the crowd, marveling at what was unfolding before him. He thought that it might take Blue the whole week to work them up this much, but no—he had done it all in a matter of hours. If the entirety of Revival Week was the same, they would all be exhausted by the last Sunday. They would be crawling to their seats, sniffling and sniveling and broken by their own rejuvenation. Maybe that was the point.

A flash of yellow caught his attention. Dallas homed in on the color, leaning forward just slightly to get a better look. It was a yellow collared shirt, interrupted by a pearly white corset that laced all the way up the front and the back like a handsomely structured vest. Abel was the one wearing it, with all their brown hair swept over one shoulder so that the pearl earring that dangled from their right lobe caught the faint light.

They were seated comfortably in one of the folded chairs with their legs crossed, one ankle resting against their opposite knee and one arm strung across the back of the neighboring chair where a woman was doubled over in her seat. She seemed unaware of her infernal neighbor. She had her face buried in her hands and her shoulders quivered with what might have been sobs or spiritual vigor, it was difficult to tell. Abel smiled at Dallas and winked. They ran their gloved hand down the woman's curved spine and she shot up. Her eyes were wild, and her hair was stuck to her tear-streaked face. Her bottom lip looked like it might have been bleeding. Dallas recognized her as Brother Rory's wife.

The noise in the revival tent seemed to dim, and it was replaced by the sound of the devil's hand going down Sister Alice's back. Suddenly, Dallas was very aware of the sound of soft leather against fabric, and the gentle grind of strands of hair slipping over one another.

"Link by link, they come undone," the devil said. Their smile widened and they tilted their chin. "Start at the bottom and work your way up."

Dallas licked his lips. "I don't have it yet," he whispered, fearing he would be overheard. "I'm not there—yet."

The devil's smile vanished as easily as it came. They buried their hand into Sister Alice's hair and took a fistful, yanking it back until her neck bowed and her chin pointed towards the ceiling. Sister Alice screamed, and Dallas almost jumped to his feet. He kicked his footrests up so he could stand while the scream sliced through the tent and numbed every tongue that stood babbling at the center near the pulpit.

A dozen eyes turned her way and Sister Alice stared back at them, as shocked as they all were. She clutched her hand against the back of her head and choked on her own words.

Abel was still sitting next to her, but no one could see them except for Dallas.

"Alice?" Brother Rory stepped away from the crowd and towards his wife. He was beet-faced and sweating, and at some point he had taken off his suit jacket. "What is wrong?"

"I felt...something," Sister Alice stammered out. "I felt something pull my hair."

"It was the devil," Dallas spoke before anything else could be said. All eyes turned to him and he could feel every one of them burning through his skin.

Yet, the only eyes that mattered were Blue's, and they were the last to turn. His reverend husband had a calm, cool gaze unlike the wide-eyed, gaping guppies that surrounded him.

"What do you mean?" Reverend Blue asked. Dallas looked down at him, meeting his eyes for what felt like the very first time.

"The devil took hold of Sister Alice, I saw it," Dallas said. "He stands by her, still. He..." His words stuck in his throat before he managed to spit them out, burdened by vitriol. "He has the form of a man, but his head is a two-faced black cat. His eyes are sickly and yellow and full of hate. Praise God."

Abel smiled again and rolled their eyes, but the expression seemed fond somehow.

"Impossible. I..." Brother Rory turned to look at Blue. "Impossible!"

Reverend Blue whipped a handkerchief out of his jacket pocket and dragged it across his forehead. "Dallas has had visions from the Holy Spirit warning him of Satan's presence," Blue said. "And the black cat was in your barn, Rory."

Brother Rory paled. He twisted around to face Dallas, his expression equal amounts of accusation and panic. Dallas raised his chin, intent on speaking for himself, but another voice interrupted—quieter, more unsure of itself.

"Sister Alice came to visit me last month when I was pregnant," a young woman spoke from her seat near the front. "Three days after she left, I bled and lost my baby. If that ain't the work of the devil, I'm not sure what is."

"Brother Rory said he would help me patch a leak in my ceiling," a man closer to the back spoke up. "They found mold in it afterwards, three inches thick."

"Sister Alice threw red brick dust on my doorstep," another testimony came.

"Sister Alice helped me can peaches and they were all rotten the next day."

"She gave my dog a nasty cough just by looking at him twice."

"She gave me a migraine just by walking by."

"Sister Alice—"

"Brother Rory—"

"Alice—"

The testimonies clamored over one another, each one louder and more panicked as they fought to be heard. Dallas sat back down and watched as Sister Alice tried to rise from her seat and bolt. She was stopped by a flurry of hands and shrieked as they all grabbed onto her. Several bodies worked together to drag her out into the center aisle, throwing her down onto the ground in front of Blue hard enough that she hit the grass face-first. Her head bounced off the ground and her nose split open, spraying blood almost a whole foot in front of her.

"Rory!" she cried out. She reached out desperately for her husband, bloody fingers splayed apart. Brother Rory stayed rooted to his spot, his face drained of all color and expression. He kept one hand tucked against his chest, fingers curled up in his tie to the point where Dallas wondered if he was trying to strangle himself.

"We cannot abide by the devil here in the House of the Lord," Blue's voice climbed above the clamor. "Satan must be driven out!"

"Cast out the devil!" the congregation echoed in unison.

"Stomp out the devil!" Blue stamped his foot against the ground.

"Stomp out the devil!" the congregation all stomped their feet to mimic him.

"Stomp on the head of the snake!" Blue's voice was not his own. It was the same dark, resonant boom that had commanded Dallas' grandfather to walk. Every emphasized word was punctured by his heel plunging down into the grass, kicking up clods of soil with threads of spittle flying from his lips.

"Cast the devil out! Stomp out the devil!" The congregation's thudding soles echoed like claps of thunder off the tent walls. They poured into the center aisle towards Sister Alice and began to kick her, striking her with the toes and sides of their shoes and stabbing her with their heels. Alice screamed in agony, each cry like a goat being bled out for slaughter. The blood on the congregation's red clothes was only visible because of how it soaked through the hems of their skirts and trouser legs. It seeped into the grass and stained every dark green blade a murderous shade of crimson. A holy color. Christ's blood, the color of sin expunged.

Bone snapped and cartilage crackled in a grisly chorus. The members fell back one by one, staggering back to their chairs in exertion. Slick fingers squealed over the metal, smearing wet trails of blood over whatever they grabbed onto. Sister Alice's body remained right where it had fallen, hardly resembling a person as much as a pile of butcher's waste.

The congregation had blood on its hands, but Reverend Blue was still clean. He tilted his head back and stretched his arms out towards Heaven, speaking half in a babbling language that Dallas could not comprehend.

"Glory to God and the Holy Spirit!" Blue's voice cracked. "This town needs Revival!"

"This town needs Revival!" the congregation echoed back.

"Blessed be the Lord our God." Blue clenched his fist and pulled it back to his chest. He squeezed his eyes shut and bowed his head, while Dallas swept his gaze over the disheveled rows of seats.

Abel was still sitting there in spotless yellow and white. Only now they were smoking a cigarette, and their brown eyes looked almost orange in the light.

CHAPTER TWELVE

HOW GREAT THOU ART

Dallas returned to the parish alone. The sermon was over, but Blue had stayed behind for a few lingering members who wanted some extra prayers after dismissal. Brother Rory was left to shovel up his wife's remains on his own. Dallas wondered if he planned to take them to the same ash pit where he had burned the two-headed kitten.

The light was on in the kitchen when Dallas stopped at the front steps. He thought he had turned everything off before leaving with Blue that morning, but apparently, he had missed one. Dallas abandoned his wheelchair at the bottom step and grasped the railing as he climbed up to the front door. Blue would have to fold it up and bring it into the house, since Dallas himself could not very well lift it.

The front door came open as soon as he touched the knob. He did not even have the chance to slide his key into the lock. Dallas' heart skipped a heavy, wet beat and he took a step back from the threshold. It could have been nothing. The house was old, after all. The light could have been left on by mistake and there was a chance that neither of them pulled the door all the way shut when leaving. However, he was tempted to sit down on the porch steps and wait for Blue all the same.

A waft of strong tobacco tickled his nose. Dallas exhaled sharply and rubbed his nostrils to try and stop himself from sneezing.

"I think the least they could do is install a ramp for you, Pastor Dallas." Abel's voice came from behind him. The devil's tongue stroked the honorific with a playfully snide, coquettish intonation.

"Maybe once Revival is over." Dallas shot them a look. "Didn't you hear that the devil is in our midst?"

"That's quite a rumor." Abel stepped a little closer and rested their hand against the porch banister. "Perhaps they have come to collect their due."

Their words squeezed all the air out of Dallas' lungs. His heart hammered weakly, as if struggling to stay in its place. "Is it the new moon, already?" he asked.

Abel glanced up towards the porch roof. There was only a flickering yellow bulb above their head. "Do you think two-headed kittens are born underneath anything else but a dead light?" they asked. "There are only stars tonight."

Dallas nodded and pressed his hand against his chest, feeling his heart drum against his palm as he tried to force himself to breathe. "Blue will be home soon," he said. "I don't know when."

"The devil works quicker." Abel winked. They slipped their fingers underneath Dallas' hand and peeled it away from his chest. They touched their lips to Dallas' wrist, then traced the prominent blue vein down his arm. When they came back up, they closed the inch of separation still between them and drew him in for a kiss.

Abel's mouth was firm, although their lips were soft and pliant. They prodded Dallas' lips with their tongue until he invited them in. Their tongue slid into his mouth—wanting, searching, and hungry. Dallas moaned, pressing his hands up against their chest and opening his mouth as wide as he could to accommodate the never-ending slide of thick muscle. Abel's tongue stretched on until it touched the back of his throat and triggered Dallas' gag reflex. His throat contracted around the devil's tongue and he half-choked, half-moaned as he clung to Abel's shirt, wrapping his fingers up in whatever pieces of the soft fabric he could grab. Dallas raised his leg and wrapped it around Abel's hip, encouraging them to grind down between his thighs while they braced their arms around him.

After a moment, it all shifted. Abel drew their tongue out of Dallas' mouth and dragged their lips over to his ear. Their throaty voice was ragged with hunger, every word coated with need that was thicker than honey.

"Let's take this to the bedroom," they said. "It will be much nicer for you in there."

They left the salacious words tickling the shell of his ear as they took a single step back. Dallas did not expect the cold, panicked wave of loneliness that crashed into him the moment their hands slid away. The absence of their body heat left him feeling desperate. Abandoned. He turned immediately back towards the door and pushed it open. Cold, moist air conditioning that circulated through the dripping unit in the living room window greeted him. It carried the lingering smell of Blue's balsam candle, even though it had been snuffed out since the night before.

Dallas reached behind him, fingers beckoning, hoping that he was being followed. Abel teased their fingertips over his arm, although they did not take his hand. Dallas led the devil to his bedroom, feeling as solemn and as close to tears as a death row prisoner. He fought the urge to throw himself down onto the ground and crawl the rest of the way. He was not familiar with that feeling—with that dark, aching hunger that twisted his belly and threatened to turn him inside-out. Abel was as calm as they could be, in comparison. And they were handsome. So goddamn handsome. They stopped just in front of the bed and stood there with all the maleficent glow of a Doré painting. Dallas made sure the bedroom door was shut and then stood just a few feet away, dying to be kissed again.

"I don't know what I'm doing." The admission came spilling out of Dallas' mouth. "It has been—only a few times."

"That is all right," Abel said. They worked the top buttons of their crisp white blouse free until the neckline met with that of the corset. "I give direction well." They swept up their long brown hair and twisted it into a knot that rested against the nape of their neck. "Most people, in your position, would kneel."

"What?" Dallas breathed and furrowed his brow.

"Kneel," the devil said sharply. Dallas dropped to his knees so hard that the impact sent a spike of pain up to his temple. He threw himself down onto his hands, copper curls spilling in every direction. He did not dare look up. The devil's tone had sent fear burrowing down into his heart, shot out like a bullet.

Fine heels made soft, thumping sounds as they tread across the carpet. The devil was circling him. A bird of prey with its eyes on a field mouse. Leather hissed against fabric and the devil's pacing stopped behind him. Dallas kept his head down, waiting, unsure of what was expected of him when he was still fully clothed.

"Sit up," the devil said. "I want you on your knees."

Dallas obeyed quickly. He sat up as straight as he could and rested his hands against his thighs, already dizzy— although it might have been a combination of the heat and the pain in his back.

A loud snap sounded off behind his head—like the smacking of a leather belt. Dallas had heard it many times before now. It brought goosebumps to his skin, but he did not move. He kept his eyes on the foot of the bed in front of him, waiting for further direction.

"Now," the devil said. "Take off your shirt."

Dallas started in on his buttons, although the holes were tight and did not want to cooperate. He managed to open his shirt up halfway down his chest before he ripped off the last few buttons. The red plastic scattered and vanished from his sight, and he ripped the rest of his shirt off down his shoulders before balling it up and tossing it aside. His binder was still on, but Abel had not said to remove it, so he hesitated.

It did not seem to matter. As soon as Dallas' shirt was off, the devil leaned over his shoulder, cooing something in his ear on a breath so soft that Dallas could not make out the words. The devil slid the leather belt along his throat, allowing the new-smelling leather to glide over his larynx and warm against his throbbing jugular. Then the belt tightened, and Dallas gasped. His hands flew to his throat and scraped instinctively against the leather, but the devil purred again in his ear.

"You do not need to be afraid," they said. They tightened the belt again and stars burst across Dallas' vision. The world in front of him began to fade into something dark and cool and it left his head buzzing with all the blood that was trapped in his face. He shivered on his knees and the entire lower half of him tightened. When he swallowed, he felt his throat expand and press up against the cruel, resisting band—and it was bliss.

"That is good," the devil crooned. "You are a very good boy." They used their free hand to stroke his cheek, sliding their thumb up and down near the corner of his mouth. Dallas tried to speak, but the words staggered out in an unintelligible groan. He could not breathe, and he did not want to. The world was spinning out of his control and bursting into colorful, bright fireworks.

Finally, the belt slackened, and Dallas gasped on a breath. It was too much for him to take in all at once and he coughed, but it was all sent back into bliss when the devil's hands ran through his hair, scratching his scalp and tugging on his curls by their roots. Dallas leaned back on his knees until he fell against the devil's chest, allowing himself to be caressed by those long, silk fingers and pointed nails. Abel's hands wandered up and down his neck, his face, and his chest, exploring every bare inch. They slid underneath the edges of his binder and then raked back down over his ribs before they could get much further. Everything between his legs was tight and quivering, needy and soaked. He was so wet that he could not think of anything else except the slick, ready warmth that glazed his cunt and soaked through his underwear.

"Take your due," Dallas managed to whisper. To his own ears his voice was needier, threadier than he would have liked. He swallowed hard and followed his words with a soft, "please."

"I always do," Abel ran their hand up his spine. "And as long as you know me, I always will."

Dallas bent back down following the path of their hand. When he was on all fours again, Abel slipped their fingers down his waistband and pulled his trousers down to his knees. Dallas bowed his head until it was pressed against the floor and the carpet was grinding against his brow. With Abel's assistance, he kicked his trousers off completely and then spread his legs as wide as he could. The devil's fingers trailed up his thighs, lingering over the hot, wet space right where the pubic hair started curling. Abel's fingers did everything except touch where he wanted it the most, and Dallas felt like he was going to fall apart.

He wanted to beg more, but he forced himself to keep his mouth shut. The devil's fingertips finally relented, stroking just the outside of his cunt. They worked back and forth, collecting more wetness and sliding up towards Dallas' hot, aching clit. Dallas cried out when the devil's fingers pressed against him, grinding down onto his clit and then slipping towards his entrance. The fingertips teased him, sliding in just enough. Dallas tried to grind down and take in more of them, but the devil kept his touch light, stroking him just a little bit more before pulling their fingers away altogether.

The belt still hung around his neck. Abel grabbed the slackened end and pulled it tight. Stars burst over Dallas vision once again and he whimpered, while at the same time feeling the devil press between his legs—hot, thick, and so very hard.

"Yes," Dallas gasped. It was a desperate, wrenching sound. "Yes, yes, yes—please, please—" his words were cut off by the belt again. The devil pulled it tight enough that he could barely breathe. Dallas wondered if it could be pulled tight enough to crush his windpipe. He wondered what it would sound like crackling underneath the leather. Every hoarse, dragging breath that came from his mouth seemed to suggest he was closer to that moment than he assumed.

Abel kept the belt wrapped around their hand, using the other to hold onto Dallas' hips as they pushed their way inside. A long, drawn-out moan dragged itself out of Dallas' throat and he pressed his face closer to the floor, flattening his cheek against the carpet. The devil filled him entirely, forcing him to spread his legs wider to accommodate the girth while pressing up against every tight, clenching wall. The devil slid their cock inside until their hips were pressed up against Dallas' ass and then they lingered, only a moment, before drawing themselves back. Feeling it all retreat was enough to make Dallas squirm. Abel allowed the belt to slacken again, and Dallas gulped down a few deep breaths as he rocked back, trying to keep the devil inside of him. Abel withdrew until they were nearly out, completely, and then they slammed back inside. A scream tore from Dallas' throat and he dug his fingers down into the carpet, bracing himself against the floor for dear life as he took every successive, titanic thrust. The devil held onto his thighs, using them as leverage while their pounding cock sent every muddled thought sliding off his tongue.

"God, God, God!" Dallas cried out. "Father in Heaven— God Almighty—oh, My God! Oh, My God!"

"Is that who you call upon?" Abel smacked his ass and then spread his cheeks apart, sliding their fingers down to touch his second entrance while still thrusting inside the other. "Does God have every finger snared in your veins? Do you belong to Him, body and soul?"

"No, no—!" Dallas moaned. "No, no, no—!"

"Of course not." Abel leaned over until their chest was touching Dallas' curved back. "You are Hell's prodigy. It is my rod, my scepter, and my throne." They rolled their hips and gave one final, hard thrust. They slammed their hips into Dallas, bearing him down onto the floor and grabbing his curls at the same time. They pushed their hand underneath him, stroking his clit while their knees kept his thighs forced apart. He was helpless beneath them and pinned so effectively that he could barely thrash. He could only submit helplessly as his orgasm climbed to its breaking point and brought tears to his eyes.

"Please, please," Dallas begged. "Please, let me, please, please, I want to, please—"

"That would be kind of me, wouldn't it?" Abel sank their teeth into Dallas' shoulder. He cried out again and bucked, pushing down onto their cock and clenching his thighs. He was not able to hold onto it. He wanted to, but he couldn't. He came without being told that he could, and he gushed onto the devil's cock and their fingers. Tears of bitter rage at his own weakness and shame came streaming from his eyes, along with trembling cries of relief. His entire body ached and shook, but it was nothing compared to the pleasure that had burst inside of him like a balloon.

Abel withdrew, slowly, stroking their hands along the side of Dallas' thighs as they did so. They shushed him, cooing softly, and stroked his curls while he settled down. He wanted to ask if they came, if they enjoyed themselves, but it was a ridiculous question. Of course they had, he could feel it. He was wetter than before, and they had left a trail down the inside of his thigh. He was filled to the brim with the devil's seed, and it spilled out when he shifted even the slightest—a communion cup with too much wine.

"There's a boy," Abel said sweetly. "There is a good, precious boy."

"I can't..." Dallas paused to get his bearings and licked his lips. "I can't move." He groaned. "Blue is going to kill me...if he finds me like this."

"He won't," the devil reassured him, sounding a little less than enthused by his worry. "Not as much time has passed as you think. Take a moment." They pressed a kiss against his temple. "Just take a moment and enjoy it."

CHAPTER THIRTEEN

IN THE HOUR OF TRIAL

A sound like a rock being thrown against glass woke Dallas up. His eyes flew open before the rest of his body could catch up, and there was a terrifying moment of stillness where all he could do was stare at the window across from him. He forced himself to take a deep breath, dragging it through his nose and pushing it out of his mouth. On the second circulation, he was able to move his arms. Another breath, and he was able to sit up.

There was a bright splatter of blood across the window's glass, seeping into a spiderweb of fine cracks created by the sudden impact. Dallas pulled his legs over the side of the bed and leaned forward to try and get a better look. On the windowsill was a scattering of soft grey and black feathers leading to a crumpled, bleeding mass—what were clearly the remains bird with one wing sticking up into the air.

Dallas reached back and grabbed Blue's side to shake him.

"Blue," he whispered. "Wake up."

Blue rolled over to face him, sliding one hand down his bare golden shoulder and pushing his saintly face into his pillow. "Good morning to you," he muttered.

"Blue." Dallas shook him again. "There is a dead bird on our windowsill."

"Is there?" Blue opened one sleepy eye. "There are plenty of cats around to take care of it."

Another thump. Dallas saw the little grey body hurl itself against the glass, but that did not stop him from yelping in surprise and slamming his hand down over his heart. Another explosion of red, and the bird went tumbling through the air. It hit the edge of the windowsill and bounced right out of view in a spray of little feathers.

Blue was out of bed in a second. He walked over to the window, the padding of his bare feet muffled by the carpet. He was still inches away from the sill when another bird came barreling into the window. It was followed almost immediately by another, and another, until they were raining against the glass like hailstones.

They burst like little bags of blood the moment they struck the surface, creating craters on the points of impact that spread more spiderweb-thin lines. The outside sill was littered with corpses of dead, grey birds with even more falling to the ground. The onslaught was so sudden and violent that it was like they were being thrown rather than crashing of their own volition.

Another bird hit the window and got snagged on the cracked glass. It screamed and thrashed, beating its wings against the window to try and rip itself free. More glass splintered and the bird slammed its head against the crater, getting its tiny head stuck in a newly made hole that sent shards of glass raining down onto the carpet. The bird died with a final, strangled chirp. Dallas could finally see the black eye-markings streaked across the soft grey head. They were butcherbirds—shrikes.

Blue spent a moment just staring at the bird caught in the window. Then he stepped closer and extended his hand, pushing his index finger against its hook-tipped beak. The head wobbled and he pinched it, wiggling it again before placing his whole hand around the head and tugging. The ligaments all disconnected with a 'pop'. The shrike's body fell to the windowsill while Blue turned to face Dallas once again. The shrike's head rested in his palm, a bloody stump that looked more like a ball of lint than anything that had been alive only minutes before. Dallas' stomach flopped and he grimaced.

"Don't touch that," he said. "It could have lice."

"Lice is not the parasite that worries me." Blue stood there with the shrike's head in his hand and blood smeared all over the sides of his palm, staring at Dallas with those knowing, cornflower blue eyes. "Do you think we made the wrong judgment yesterday?"

Indignance and fear made a nauseating cocktail in his empty stomach. Dallas raised his chin.

"What do you mean?" he asked. It came out more challenging than he intended.

Blue turned his eyes back to the bird's head. "The devil is still among us," he said. "That much is clear. Did we name the wrong usurper?" His voice held a thread of uncertainty.

Dallas realized his choice. If he did not double down, he would lose his credibility as a vessel of the Holy Spirit. Furthermore, he could not allow Blue to humanize himself to the congregation. The question was a rare moment of vulnerability—a gift, as far as Dallas was concerned, in his own case. But for the church, Blue had to remain larger than a myth. Admitting any mistake would bring him down in their collective eyes, and then they would pick him apart and question everything. It would all inevitably fall apart after that.

It happened to every pastor, eventually, if they lost hold of their flock. Blue would be ushered out. A new reverend would be brought in. And if Blue left, then Dallas would have to go too—and no one would burn. No one would pay. Sister Alice's blood was not payment enough. Her death was only the first stone that had been cast.

Dallas pushed himself off the side of the bed and stood, moving closer to Blue. He cupped his hand underneath the reverend's, allowing it to hover in mid-air, not quite touching.

"Are you questioning the Holy Spirit?" Dallas asked.

Blue raised his chin. "No," he said. "The Holy Spirit is absolute."

"The devil is a usurper," Dallas hammered on. "When Jesus cast the devil into swine, it was the entire herd that ran into the water. One of our number has died, but that does not mean the devil has been cast out. If anything, he has taken root in multiple doubting hearts." Dallas clasped Blue's hand all the sudden between both of his, closing the reverend's fingers over the dead bird's head. "He must be scraped out like an infection. Nothing missed, or he will continue to spread until he has taken them all."

Blue squeezed his hand. Small bones crackled underneath his strong fingers. "This is why Revival is so important," he said. Dallas smiled.

"Exactly," he agreed.

"We must pray," Blue told him. "We need to ask God for strength today, for we are marching into an unprecedented battle."

"Yes," Dallas said. He glanced down at their hands and wondered over a sudden spark of inspiration. "Let me pray over you," he added. "Let the Holy Spirit grant you atonement for your doubt."

Blue nodded his agreement. He pulled his hand free and cast the shrike's head aside. Then he sank down to his knees while Dallas paced behind him, going for the simple dresser and for what he knew was in the top drawer.

"Begin your prayers," Dallas said. He did not host the Voice of God and he did not have the devil's sultry presence, but Blue obeyed him, all the same. The reverend began a prayer as fervent as if he was standing behind a pulpit. He lifted his hands to Heaven and hung his head low between his raised arms. Every tense muscle rippled across his golden, tanned back where his shoulder-blades jutted out like an archangel's wings.

Dallas reached into Blue's top dresser drawer and pulled out his belt. It was simple and black but made of good and expensive leather. Dallas made a loop and then wrapped the rest around his hand before moving to stand behind the reverend. He splayed his legs apart and set his hand against Blue's back just to feel the muscles twitch. Blue's voice caught with the touch, but he did not slow in his prayers. Dallas ground his back teeth and began to pray as well, picking up on the thread of Blue's tone and matching the heat with his own.

As he prayed, Dallas raised the belt and then paused before bringing it down across Blue's back. Leather hit flesh with a sharp, bright sound and left behind a wide pink stripe that looked like it had been painted on. Blue's prayer skipped like a record that had been jolted, but he did not stop. If anything, he began to pray harder, thrusting his hands towards the sky and dipping his head even lower.

Dallas brought the belt down against the reverend's back again and again. His inexperienced blows felt choppy, not all of them landing where he desired. Some of them bounced off the side of Blue's head or smacked against his ribs, but the reverend did not seem to mind. Dallas kept praying, although he lost track of his own words in trying to focus on landing more even blows. Blue's back became a landscape of pink and wine-red stripes, with a smear or two of blood in places where multiple blows had struck and broken the skin.

At last, Dallas' arm became too tired to continue. He lowered it down to his side and gripped the back of Blue's neck, keeping the reverend's head down while he finished out his prayer. On Blue's final words, he reached behind his head and grasped Dallas' hand. The reverend's skin was feverishly hot, and his sudden grip was like encountering a stovetop burner coil.

As suddenly as he had launched into them, Blue ceased his prayers. He sat on his knees, trembling, soaking in the quiet moment and wiping at his mouth with his bloody hand. Dallas kissed the back of his blond head and straightened.

"I will get you some water from the kitchen," Dallas said.

Blue nodded and raised his head.

"I feel God's grace," he said. "Today has been promised to us."

"So do I," Dallas agreed before walking out of the bedroom. His hand still throbbed from the belt, similarly to his neck from the night before.

CHAPTER FOURTEEN

AND CAN IT BE THAT I SHOULD GAIN

Breakfast was homemade biscuits oozing with golden cheese and individually wrapped in foil to trap the heat. Next to their heap was a mountain of country sausage patties that were far more exposed, and they were losing steam faster than a Tupperware salesman. The sausage and the country-fried steaks had been donated by Brother Hugh, who butchered his own meat and sold it in his own shop for a considerably inflated 'market value'. There was no doubt that he saw the merit in donating to a higher cause, but Dallas still did not have a lot of confidence in the selection that was being offered. After all, there was nothing to say that the man had not simply pulled all the expired product from his shelves and unloaded it as a tax write-off. At any rate, the edges of all the patties were suspiciously hard and black. Brother Lionel made a joke about burnt offerings and Brother Hugh laughed about it.

Dallas took two biscuits from their pile and plopped them down onto his paper plate. Sister Marge Elsie eyed him from her place near the beverages. When he approached, the smile she gave him was entirely false.

Marge Elsie hovered her hand over the caps of the jugs in front of her. "Good morning, Pastor Dallas," she said. "Would you like some apple juice? Or we have fresh coffee."

Fresh was a matter of opinion that he was not willing to argue. "Just some apple juice for me," he said. "Thank you, sister." He kept his gaze level with hers. Dallas hated looking anyone in the eye, except when it was a challenge. Marge Elsie's were wet, slimy little hazel globes that only reflected her empty smile.

She passed him a red plastic cup. The apple juice was not very cold, but he was glad to have it anyway. Dallas finally did drop his gaze so that he could focus on nestling the cup between his thighs and balancing his plate on his knees so that he could move his wheelchair towards a table.

"Today is going to be a good day," he muttered, trying to leave her with some cordial parting words. "I feel the Lord's presence among us already."

"I hope that is true," Marge Elsie said without missing a beat. "I feel we are all in desperate need of today's sermon.

And," she glanced at Blue, "the reverend is not looking too well."

Her patronizing tone made Dallas clench his jaw. Oh, she hated him. It was spelled out clear as day in her voice. He wanted to tell the old bitch that it was mutual—that when it was her turn to give up the ghost in the church aisles he would be particularly interested in the spectacle. The disparity in her gaze from how she looked at him to how she regarded Blue was astonishing. But then, she knew nothing about the quarter-sized bruise that was barely concealed by the reverend's high collar with Dallas' teeth marks in the center. She had not seen his bright, cold eyes glazed over in pleasure and she had never seen his flushed face drenched in slick, pearly sin. Dallas wondered what she would think if she could see Blue that way.

An hour earlier, before Blue washed his face and dragged a comb through his neat blond hair, he had looked like all that and worse. He and Dallas had neglected to leave as they meant to right after prayer, and Dallas had ridden Blue's face on their bedroom floor while staring at a window of broken glass and dead shrikes.

He wanted to tell her. He wanted to look her in the eye and say "I fucked him. I fucked your reverend until he blasphemed in my name. And then he buried his face between my legs and worshiped me with his tongue. You should be grateful that he has enough water left in him to deliver today's sermon."

Dallas didn't say it, because he knew she would not understand. Marge Elsie was the sort who probably wouldn't know an orgasm if it jumped up and smacked her in the cunt.

He realized he was staring at her. Not in the eyes, but somewhere around her chin. He knew that she was staring back at him, though, completely unafraid.

She did not know that she had any reason to be afraid of him, not yet. She must not have been paying attention the night before when Sister Alice was beaten into the grass like a copperhead snake. That was Dallas' doing. Anyone could try and deny it, but the truth was irrefutable. Blue might have been the voice, but Dallas was his Elohim. It was Dallas who pointed the damning finger.

He turned his head away without saying anything else and moved to a table where no one else was sitting. He unwrapped his sandwich and let it sit there in the malleable foil. Brown, crispy cheese stuck to some of the creases and the biscuit fell apart when he tried to pull it up. Dallas wrapped some of the boiling cheese around his fingers and stuck a heap in his mouth. He did not care that it burned the roof or that it seared his bitten lips while passing through. He shoved another bite in before the first one was even complete, chewing it all at once before swallowing derisively and pushing his fingers down into the center of the remaining crumpled biscuit.

'The reverend is not looking too well.' Her words bounced off the sides of his muddled brain. It was clear to him that she had never seen anyone so well-fucked. She had no idea about the blood-vessels that could burst underneath the eyes and the dark circles that could surface when one was being held face-down against the floor. Exhaustion and exhilaration shared a color palette.

She would know that, if she ever spent time away from the church pews, but she did not. Dallas wondered if she carried anything in her purse to do the job in the middle of morning service. A little handheld flashlight, probably. It would put a whole different spin on her famous speech of several Sundays ago, where she had stood up in the middle of service and screamed about 'God's light shining deep within her'. The thought made Dallas laugh out loud and choke on his biscuit.

A paper plate, overburdened by sausage patties and wet yellow scrambled eggs, landed on the table as Blue sat down. Dallas' eyes widened and he threw a look around, feeling a little bit like he was about to be reprimanded for laughing at his private thoughts—like all the times his grandfather had caught him falling asleep in church.

"You need to eat a little more than that," Blue nodded at Dallas' plate. "You'll be keeling over before we finish Amazing Grace."

"Sausage makes me sweat," Dallas said. He stole a patty off Blue's plate anyway and tore it in half, biting the end off one piece and setting the other down on top of his decimated biscuit. "Mm. Tastes like second-best."

"Brother Hugh was very kind to make his donation." The shadow of a smile played across Blue's lips. "And it serves the Lord to not waste His bounty."

"That's a very sweet way of saying that this sausage tastes a little sour." Dallas bit off another chunk. "Not that you can tell much underneath the char."

Blue's smile transformed into something a bit more tangible as he picked up a Styrofoam cup of coffee. "You know," he said, "I have yet to see you cook."

"I can cook," Dallas said, feeling somewhat indignant. "It just seems a shame to deprive your disciples of the pleasure."

Blue shook his head. "My mother..." He paused. The sudden lull lent an unexpected gravity to half-finished words. As many times as he had told the miraculous story of his birth, as far as Dallas was concerned, Reverend Blue had no mother. He had simply risen from the ground one day, fully-formed and ready to take the pulpit. The veneer was flaking off, bit by bit, like layers of gilded paint covering ugly rust.

Dallas held Blue's gaze, silently urging him to finish. Blue pushed his eggs around his paper plate and then shoveled them into his mouth. He chewed over them thoughtfully before he continued. "My mother did not do much cooking, either," he said. "We ate a lot of microwaved meals. Mind you," he waved his fork somewhat airily, "the microwave was a gift. We could never afford anything like that on our own."

Dallas sat with that image for a minute. Not just Blue with a mother, but Blue with a poor mother. Blue without the shining Rolex and the dangling earrings and the mouthful of white teeth that cost more than most folks' rent. Blue eating beef Manhattans and practicing all his sermons from a well-loved family Bible.

By the time Dallas pulled himself back to the present, the reverend had shuttered his expression again and was cleaning his plate. It was almost a relief. The moment had been too revealing for either of them to bear.

"I'll take your plate," Dallas said when Blue stood up to leave. The reverend just nodded and set his hand on Dallas' shoulder before walking away.

There was still a red stain in the grass where the devil had been stomped out of Sister Alice. Brother Rory was late to the Revival service, and he could not seem to look anyone in the eye as he slid into the only empty seat on the end of the second row. His hands trembled when they held up the hymnal and his voice cracked as he started to sing. About halfway through How Great Thou Art was when he broke down into tears, and then he seemed desperate not to draw attention to himself. He simply closed the hymnal and tucked it underneath his metal chair as he sat down. He pulled out a white handkerchief and dug the corner into his eyes, collecting the tears and catching the trail of snot that tried to race out of his quivering nostrils. Dallas watched every movement, fascinated—even more so because from where he sat, Brother Rory's foot rested right on the edge of his wife's stain.

At last, the hymns died down and the congregation took their seats. Their backsides clapped thunderously against the metal folding chairs, and then following the din was a long stretch of silence. Dallas waited for Blue to speak, but he kept his eyes on Rory. The older man's leg was bouncing, too full of anxiety to stay still. His veiny red hand clutched his knee until his knuckles went pale and he began to rock back and forth, slamming his free hand down onto his thigh like he was in pain. Yet, he was nodding the whole time Reverend Blue spoke, while his whole face glistened with snot, sweat, and tears in one place or another.

A flash of yellow appeared in Dallas' peripherals. He turned his head, half-expecting to see the devil walking up and down the rows, stepping over knees and straddling thighs. The only thing his eyes landed on was a wide sunhat with a yellow ribbon tied around the middle. The floppy brim was tilted down too low for him to make out much of the wearer's features.

"Reverend!" Brother Rory snapped Dallas' attention back to the rows. He stood with one hand stretched towards Heaven, the other resting on his wide leather belt. "Reverend, I have something that I need to say to the congregation here today!"

Reverend Blue turned his cold, steely eyes towards Brother Rory and spread his hands. He brought them to rest on either side of the temporary pulpit and leaned forward so that his lips were almost touching the microphone clipped onto the front. "You have the floor, Brother Rory," Blue said. "What has the Lord put on your heart today?"

Brother Rory straightened his back and shifted his gaze until he was staring right at Dallas. Even with a few yards between them, Dallas could feel his hatred. It swam around his red-rimmed eyes that had probably not slept the night before. It eked out the sides of his mouth which refused to close, as if each labored breath came hard-won, and his nose was too stopped up for the exhale.

"I have been a Christian all my life," Brother Rory said. "My mother raised us on the good book and sent us to bed reciting verses. I walked through those church doors every time they were open to dwell in the house of the Lord and give Him praise. And then Alice..." he paused, choking on the words before forcing himself to continue. "...Alice wasn't never any different. She was a good Christian woman, and I never caught her straying from the righteous path, not once. Now, I've been up all night, pastor. I've been praying. And God never said to me, Rory, your Alice is burning in Hell for being a witch. In fact, God's been a bit quiet this whole time. And I started thinking of the last time I felt God—I mean really felt God's presence—and I don't think it's been since Brother Andy died. Now, I'm not saying there's been any foul play. But all I know is that Andy Hackett died when he was dancing and hollering and praising the Lord. Something that I don't think everyone who is here could stand to see. Do you get my meaning, Pastor?"

It was clear that he was not talking to Blue anymore. Dallas drew in a deep breath at the mention of his grandfather. The quick expansion from his lungs sent a stitch of pain up his side, and he set his hand against his ribs as he tried to breathe through it.

"I cannot speak for the state of Sister Alice's heart or mind," Reverend Blue said at last. "That is between her soul and God."

Brother Rory did not say anything, and his gaze did not waver. Dallas' eyes darted towards the wide-brimmed sun hat again. The hat tilted up just enough that he could finally catch a glimpse of the face underneath. He saw a flash of twin white circles, like a light shining straight onto the eyes of an alligator at night. The white faded out into rich, dark brown, and Abel's smile curled like a cat's at the corners. Dallas froze, digging his jagged nails into the side of his knee. The devil parted their lips and another spot of yellow as bright as a banana emerged from the black space between the two swollen mounds of pink flesh. It turned into the pointed face of a yellow cobra, beady black eyes and all. Its head rested between their front teeth, and its black tongue flickered out, wobbling through the air like a ribbon.

The moment the snake appeared, Rory held his hand up to cover a fiery belch. It rumbled all the way up his chest and came tearing out, violently obtrusive as it squeezed out between his fingers.

Dallas' nail beds ached. When he opened his mouth to speak, his jaw tried to lock in protest. Until that moment, he had not even been paying attention to how hard he was clenching it.

"They make their tongues as sharp as a serpent's; the poison of vipers is on their lips." His words came out as a whisper. He did not feel capable of making them any louder.

Blue turned his head. He was gripping his bible tightly against his chest, his index finger stuck between the gilded pages he had been prepared to read from. "What did you say?" the reverend asked. Dallas continued to repeat the words, but they only came faster, not louder.

"They make their tongues as sharp as serpent's; the poison of vipers is on their lips. They make their tongues as sharp as serpent's; the poison of vipers is on their lips—" As he spoke, the yellow cobra in Abel's mouth slid out, revealing itself inch by inch—black spots and all. It reared its head and flared its hood, and at the same time, Brother Rory belched again. It was a wetter sound than the last. He plastered his hand against his mouth like he was holding back vomit.

"The poison of vipers is on their lips," Dallas hissed. Brother Rory's eyes rolled up again towards the pulpit. He pulled his trembling hand away and retched again. His mouth dropped open and Dallas caught a flash of white, like he was hiding an egg behind his teeth.

Dallas grabbed the rims of his wheels and pushed himself closer to the edge of the plywood platform. "And the great dragon was cast out." He shredded every word through his clenched teeth. "That old serpent called the Devil, and Satan, which deceiveth the whole world!" His voice finally broke free of its whisper and climbed to a sudden, shrieking height. There wasn't a whisper or murmur throughout the entire congregation, then. They hung on his every word. He watched Brother Rory gag again, watched the older man's entire chest convulse with terrible pressure that made his entire body jolt. "He was cast out into the earth," Dallas thrust out his chin. "And his angels were cast out with him."

"And his angels were cast out!" Reverend Blue echoed. The congregation's heads came up, and their eyes were all on Brother Rory. The man was pouring sweat. It streamed down the sides of his face like a bucket of water had been dumped onto his head. He grabbed onto the seat in front of him and hunched over, but Dallas could still see his eyes. They were wide enough to flash the whites and bulging as big as golf balls ready to roll out of his head. Another good retch sent a long, grey rope as thick as a country sausage sliding out of his mouth. Brother Rory's eyes rolled up and he rocked on his feet, but he vomited again and more of the sausage came out. The mottled surface was plated in fine, dark veins while a thin coating of blood lubricated its exit. Dallas' eyes darted between Rory and the devil. The yellow serpent was still coming, its coils seemingly never-ending. While every jolt and tortured hack from Rory seemed horrible enough to be his last, but the length—of what Dallas assumed by now to be intestine—kept coming.

"And his angels were cast out," Dallas' voice dropped back down to a whisper. His nails bit into his knee even through his trouser fabric. "The old serpent called the Devil, the poison of vipers is on their lips!" He wanted to close his eyes and turn his head, but he did not. He saw the yellow serpent's tail flicker as it dropped out of Abel's mouth, and at the same time Brother Rory keeled over. A mile of sausage-grey intestine was coiled at his feet and there was probably more he had not spat out, but his cheeks and eyes were bulging and his nose was leaking yellow bile. He did not look like he could breathe. He fell to the ground and landed almost on top of the very place his wife had died. Dallas supposed it was ironic, in a way.

Reverend Blue looked at him again. There was something else on his expression, this time, something Dallas had never seen there before. It could have been respect or some other mutuality. Whatever it was, it did not last for longer than a few seconds. Blue walked over to where Dallas was sitting and rested a hand on his shoulder, reining the bewildered congregation in with a word.

"Amen," Blue said. "Let's pick up our hymnals and turn to page 235. Amazing Grace, let's sing it loud today, church. This is why we need Revival, this is why we need to welcome the Lord with open arms. Sin will purge itself from our numbers if we make it known to the devil that he is not welcome here today, can I get an amen?" He stamped his foot for emphasis, and Dallas slammed his hand down on top of Blue's, squeezing the reverend's fingers.

"Amen! Hallelujah!" The congregation echoed back. Their voices shook uncertainly, at first, but strengthened after they picked up their hymnals and launched into the familiar verses. Brother Rory's body already smelled awful, and Dallas could not imagine what it would be like if left to bake in the summer heat. He had no doubt that Blue would have it all cleared away before lunch, but even if it was just for the duration of a few choruses, an engorged body buried under its own stinking bowels was nothing he wanted to see.

Dallas tried to find Abel in the crowd again, but when he saw the sun hat again, it was on the head of Sister Marge Elsie.

CHAPTER FIFTEEN

HOLY, HOLY, HOLY

"Judgment is upon us, Blue." Their bedroom window was still covered in blood, but Dallas had vacuumed up all the broken glass from the floor. Blue had cut open a trash bag and taped it down so that nothing else could get in, and now the plastic bubbled ominously whenever a breeze pushed its way through.

"Us?" Blue echoed back. He joined Dallas near the side of the bed, kneeling on the floor rather than sitting down beside him. He looked especially handsome in that moment, Dallas hated to admit. There was something about the way Blue wore his shirt with the sleeves rolled up to his elbows and the first few buttons of the collar undone. His black suspenders hugged his broad chest but were pulled tighter than a guitar string over the deep arch of his lower back. This was the version of Blue that Dallas liked the most. It was the almost-human version. The down-to-earth, blonde-haired, blue-eyed Southern boy with sun-kissed cheeks and a pouty bottom lip. In another life, Dallas could see them sitting on the same bleached-wood porch, sipping sweet tea with just a drop of moonshine and watching the sunset together. Another life where Blue was just a man, and Dallas did not want him dead.

Blue touched Dallas' back. Everything spinning thought came to a screeching halt.

"What do you mean?" Blue prompted. Dallas sucked on his teeth.

"You saw what happened to Brother Rory," he said. "The congregation should have fallen to their knees and screamed. They should have mourned. They should have torn us apart for allowing it to happen."

"They would not," Blue said. He sounded slightly irate. "God speaks through us."

"God is testing their limits," Dallas insisted. "Like water in the cracks of a stone. When the stone breaks, the water flows through, and there is no repairing the damage. We are the stones." He pushed his hand through Blue's short hair. "We are going to lose our control."

Blue was quiet for a moment. He seemed to enjoy Dallas' fingers running through his hair. He sat there on his knees, his eyes half-closed, before he took Dallas' wrist and pulled his hand down to kiss his ruddy knuckles.

"'Mine eyes do fail with tears, my bowels are troubled, my liver is poured upon the earth'." Blue looked up at last.

"That is Lamentations. 'Behold, O Lord, for I am in distress. I have grievously rebelled, at home there is as death.'"

"Brother Rory's bowels are troubled, not mine," Dallas retorted.

"Exactly so," Blue said. "God is the one who passes judgment, Dallas, and we are only the vessels of His word. We cannot think of it any other way. The congregation knows this as well as we do. Rory and Alice are a tragedy, yes, but if they strayed and allowed the devil into their hearts—did they not deserve to be cast out, and thrown upon the sword?"

Dallas caught himself staring for a little too long into Blue's cornflower eyes. They gazed back up at him, unwavering, while Blue's fingers stroked the small of Dallas' back gently.

"If they were to turn against us, do you have faith that God would hold them back?" Dallas asked. He could not help himself.

"Without a doubt," Blue said.

Dallas had no choice but to accept that answer. He nodded and pushed his hand through Blue's hair again, playing with the blunt blonde strands.

"Tell me something I don't know about you," Dallas said. "Tell me about your mother."

"My mother?" Blue sounded surprised. He shifted until he was on his knees in front of his husband and Dallas parted his thighs to allow him closer.

"Yes." Dallas laid back on the bed. Blue lowered his head and pulled down Dallas' trousers in order to kiss the warm space between his thighs. He darted his tongue up the treacherous arterial line, and the hot, slick flicker was enough to make Dallas' legs quiver with pleasure.

"She died when I was eleven," Blue said. "There isn't very much to tell."

Dallas swallowed. "Mine left when I was twelve," he said. "Isn't it strange how these things go?"

"Some animals eat their young," Blue said. "With that mind, we should probably count ourselves lucky."

Dallas sighed. Blue's tongue pressed against his underwear, warming the spot and soaking it through the longer it lingered. Blue dragged his tongue up and down in long, slow licks. The soft fabric wrinkled underneath the motion and brushed against Dallas' hot, sore clit—pulling a needy moan out of his throat.

"Cuckoo birds don't," Dallas breathed. The reverend did not respond. Blue slipped his finger through one of the legs of Dallas' underwear, pulling it to the side and exposing his slick, pink entrance. Blue pressed his tongue to the opening, gliding it up and down, skating over his clit and then diving back down towards his hole before burying his face entirely.

It was apparent that Blue was no longer interested in conversation. It was just as well. Dallas' thoughts spilled away one by one, melting into the heady whimpers that clawed for freedom from his throat.

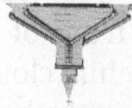

The moon in Dallas' dreamscape was bright orange, and it bathed the church in light like holy fire. The white revival tent soaked it up as well, while its nether side cast a long black shadow like a pool of melted tar. The whole world was those two colors: fire and tar. The blood on Dallas' hands looked black, but he knew it was blood. It smelled like pennies and it made his fingers stick together. Old blood, congealing blood.

In the same dream, he saw a dog. It was no bigger than his shoe and sat in front of the revival tent, black and puffy like a cotton ball. It had one brown eye and one white, with a deep scar running through the white one, splitting the side of its face open. Dallas tried to approach it, but the dog sprang up and dashed on stick-thin legs towards the tent. Dallas followed it inside while the darkness pulled him in, swallowing every spare inch of his vision until he couldn't see anything at all. He could not see anything, he could not hear anything, but he could still feel the blood on his hands. It pilled up on his skin when he rubbed his palms together. He pushed his fingers through one another and scraped his nails over his knuckles, trying to slough it off.

"Little dog?" Dallas called out. His voice sounded small and lost, like the darkness was eating it. "Come out of there, won't you? What are you doing?" As he spoke, he pushed his fingers inside his own mouth and fished around his back teeth. He grabbed hold of them and wiggled a few, unnerved by exactly how loose they were.

One of his teeth cracked free from its root and he knew that if he pulled too hard, it would come right out. He didn't want his tooth to come out. He wanted it to stay right where it was. But even more around it were loose. If he pulled out one, how many would follow? He could keep going until his mouth was full of nothing but blood and teeth.

Suddenly, a flash of gold light pierced through the darkness, and its rays filled the revival tent with searing heat like the blades of a thousand blazing swords. Dallas screamed in agony and jerked his hand out of his mouth to throw over his eyes. He collapsed to his knees and doubled over in pain until his forehead was touching the cold, hard ground.

"You must not do that," a voice spoke to him. It sounded familiar, and also like many voices speaking to him at once. Male and female, all the tongues of the congregation coming together to shape the same words. "I am a servant of the Lord. The same as you."

Dallas raised his head and cupped his hand over his brow to shield his eyes from some of the awful light. "I am no one," he said. Even as the words left his mouth, he was struck with fear. If this was an angel, or some other divine messenger, then it would be able to see into his heart and know him for what he truly was. It would be able to comb through every wrinkle in his brain like the pages of a book and see how, and when, he had made his pact with the devil. Maybe that was why it was here. Maybe he was to be punished.

He wondered what it would be like, to be smitten by an angel of the lord. He was on his knees long enough to think about it while fishing his wiggling tooth out with the tip of his tongue. It finally came loose and his mouth filled with warm, fresh blood. He spat it out, tooth and all, onto the ground.

"Be not afraid of me," the voices rose, and light continued to fill the tent. Dallas' blood was bright red on the dry grass underneath him. The ugly, broken tooth with its exposed root rested there, too, and mocked him.

Dallas finally looked up. He could not make out all the details, but it might have been an angel. It looked human enough, suspended perfectly still in the air with its arms outstretched and its feet folded over each other—like Christ nailed to the cross. He caught glimpses of long, dark hair and six golden rings, each the size of a cornfield and overlapping as they spun. The rings were thick, he could see that much, and heavily engraved. Every inch of their outer sides was covered in mismatched sets of unblinking eyes, each one as wide as his hand. Of the humanoid figure in the center, the only other detail he could make out were a pair of massive brown speckled wings. They spanned as long as the tent was wide, and all the places where the light shone through the tips made the deepest browns look bright orange.

"I am not afraid of you," Dallas finally said. He dragged his tongue over his lips and all he could taste was blood. "What message do you have for me?"

The golden rings hummed loudly as they swept through the air. "Remember Haman," the voices said, each struggling to be louder than the other until they were nearly impossible to understand. "Hanged on the gallows he built for another man. Remember the whispers of the deceiver tie their tongue in wicked knots."

Dallas wanted to speak, but he could not summon the words. His tongue was too occupied by uprooting his other teeth. He felt around his mouth for crevices until he found one that he could push his tongue into. His teeth wiggled out easily, and he spat them out as they came up. The angel of the Lord was trying to speak to him, to warn him, but he could not stop tearing up his own mouth.

"The deceiver ensnares," the voices hissed. "They will choke the holy truth out of you."

Something was crawling up his throat. Dallas felt it climbing up the back of his tongue, using pincers as sharp as new fishhooks. Dallas opened his mouth and gagged, retching as he tried to fling the thing out and spit it up. His tongue bowed in the middle and blood poured out of his gaping mouth.

"The holy truth!" the voices screamed in unison. Dallas gagged again and it was an awful, hacking sound. He wrapped his hand around his throat, as if he could squeeze the intruder out, and spat up even more blood onto the grass. All the blood trickling off his tongue was making him light-headed. And he was so hot, so hot—his eyes ached. His tongue hurt. He hacked again and it sounded like a barking dog.

It was the middle of the night, and Blue was coughing. The hard, wet sound pulled Dallas out of his nightmare, and he caught himself half-hovering over the edge of the bed with his face towards the floor. He had been spitting in his sleep, if the dark wet spot on the carpet was any indication. A copper curl was stuck to the side of his mouth and he peeled it up while brushing back the rest of his hair. Dallas' shoulders burned as he pushed himself back onto the bed and rolled over onto his side. Blue sat up at the same time, shoving his pillow down so that bunched up to support his back and brought his hand up just in time to smother another gust. Dallas could not see much of him in the dark, but he sounded awful—like that barking dog in his dream.

"Do you need some water?" Dallas asked, smearing the sleep out of his eyes. Blue shook his head and pounded his fist against his chest.

"I'm just hot," he said hoarsely. "Turn the fan on." He gestured towards the ceiling fan, but it was already whirring above their heads.

Dallas sat up on his knees anyway and reached to grab the dangling pull-chain. Two tugs and the fan blades were spinning at full speed. He returned to his place beside Blue and set the back of his hand against the reverend's forehead.

"You're burning up," he said. "What happened to you?"

"I must have eaten something that didn't agree with me," Blue said. He coughed again and let out a miserable, whining groan. "I'll be fine."

Dallas sucked on his teeth but did not say anything else. He slid off the side of the bed and walked around towards the bathroom. Blue continued to hack behind him as he filled a plastic cup full of water from the sink and then brought it to his husband, pushing it into his hand until Blue finally accepted it.

Blue nodded his thanks and drank deeply from the cup. Dallas crawled back into bed and pulled up just one blanket to slip underneath. His side was also soaked in sweat.

"If you are still sick in the morning, maybe you shouldn't preach," Dallas said. "You can barely talk now."

"I'm fine," Blue repeated, his words terser than before. "I just need to get some rest." Blue sagged against the headboard and tilted his head back to rest against it. Another cough racked his whole body, and Dallas turned away so that he at least didn't feel like he was breathing any of it in.

When he went back to sleep, he didn't dream of anything except the half-blind dog sitting on his chest and barking in his face.

CHAPTER SIXTEEN

GO TELL IT ON THE MOUNTAIN

Dallas was up with the dawn the next morning, not that Blue gave him much of a choice. His cough worsened overnight, and by the time the numbers on the digital clock triggered its alarm, Dallas had given up on sleep and was in the kitchen making tea.

Blue kept loose bags of ginger and honey tea in a glass jar that he had labelled 'remedy' with a marker and some masking tape. He also kept fresh honey-wheat bread stored in a breadbox on his counter, which took Dallas forever to find. After rooting around in the kitchen for all the plates and utensils he had not yet needed to find, he managed to dutifully prepare some hot tea and buttered toast. It was a quiet and familiar domesticity that was somewhat soothing in its own right, more so than it had a right to be. Revival had come so quickly and in the heat of it all, he had not yet found the time to settle into his own home. His bags, what little he had brought from his grandfather's house, were still barely unpacked in the corners of the bedroom. There just had not been any time.

Maybe after everything was said and done. Maybe after Revival Week had ended.

The morning light made Blue look even worse. When Dallas brought his breakfast to him, the reverend looked like he had been face-down in a sink full of water for the majority of the night.

Dallas set the reverend's mug and plate down on the bedside table and felt his forehead again. Blue's skin was clammy and his light eyes were buried underneath puffy dark circles. Whenever he tried to speak he would only wheeze before launching a wad of phlegm into the bunched-up tissues in his hand.

"Oh, yeah," Dallas said. "You are not going anywhere. That is for sure."

Blue gargled his words, a sound like he was trying to growl around a mouthful of glass, before he coughed into his tissue again. He paused after that, holding up one finger, and then cleared his throat again before turning to face Dallas.

"It is Revival," Blue rasped. "I have to be there." He could barely raise his voice above a whisper.

A cold stream of fear cut through Dallas' veins and caused goosepimples to pop up on his arms. He rubbed them, hoping the friction would smooth him out—but it did not stop the bone-deep chill that made his stomach flutter.

"Yes," Dallas agreed. "You have to be there." There were twin edges to this knife. Either Blue walked into that tent shivering, hacking up a lung, and looking like a man that God had turned away from—or he did not appear at all, and doubt started burrowing through the congregation like hookworms.

It did not take much. All the devil needed was an inch. Dallas knew firsthand what they could do with it.

"I will lead the service today," Dallas said. "I can do it. They would expect me to, anyway."

Blue made a face. "You don't have anything prepared." He coughed again into his handkerchief, violently enough that his face turned dark red.

"I have your notes," Dallas said. "I can fill in the rest. It's not brain surgery, is it?"

A muscle jumped in Blue's jaw. "I just need some more rest," he said. "I'll be better by tonight. Lead them into song...or something...maybe testimonials until lunch. Don't go in over your head."

"I don't think you need to be talking to me about going in over my head," Dallas said. "Just worry about yourself." He adjusted Blue's pillows behind him so that his back had more support. "Eat your breakfast, drink your tea, get some sleep."

"If you need anything..." Blue's words were interrupted by another coughing fit.

Dallas handed him the box of tissues from the bedside table. "I'll be fine," he said. "It's not the end of the world."

Mountains of hashbrowns and eggs were being scooped out onto paper plates while the damp early-morning August air carried the smell of black coffee up the nostrils of everyone who crowded in the reception hall kitchen. Dallas was alone in the revival tent. He stood on the platform behind Blue's pulpit, his hands stuck in his pockets as he stared down the aisle that had been formed between the folding chairs. A maelstrom of gnats had kicked up in the grass and they buzzed around Dallas' shoes. A hundred insignificantly busy little bodies that had no purpose in life other than to mark the presence of rot. Those were the only places that Dallas ever saw them, when it was around rotting fruit, rotting food, or rotting roadkill.

"You're going to lose them all." The soft, dusky voice that drifted from the front of the tent was so familiar, now. Dallas' lip curled and he looked up.

"What do you mean by that?" he asked.

Abel walked down the aisle, looking a touch underdressed in crisp white slacks and with the sleeves of their yellow dress shirt rolled up to their elbows. Their white suit jacket was draped over their shoulders like a cape with the sleeves dangling free. Their autumn-brown eyes peered at Dallas from over the rimless edges of slim sunglass lenses small enough to be pills.

They came to a stop at the end of the aisle, their gloved hand resting on the back of a metal chair.

"They don't believe in you," the devil said. "Their faith in your man is starting to waiver, too."

"How do you know that?" Dallas demanded.

"I know a doubting heart like the soil knows the worms that keep it rich." Abel smiled. "I can feel all their little concerns writhing and burrowing, searching for a grain of reassurance. Revivals are hard on the soul. They make one feel ugly and wretched at the best of times. Now, it's hardly your man's fault that these past few days have left him whupped. But his congregation has been questioning a few of his decisions, wondering if their god would approve of all this death."

Dallas gripped the sides of the pulpit. "You're trying to get me to doubt myself," he said. "If the whole flock backslides, it's better for you, isn't it?"

Abel's smile spread. "The sheep are not really my concern." They dragged out every syllable with that Old Hollywood cadence. "I come to you to collect, whether their asses are in the pews or not."

"I need their asses in the pews," Dallas spat through gritted teeth. "Like I need their suffering. Is that not what I bargained for? Is that not what you offered me?"

Abel tilted their head. "I have been holding up my end the entire time, Dallas Hackett." Their soft words were suddenly sharp and inflexible as fractured glass. "I am a little concerned that you are the ones who do not have the guts to see it all through."

Dallas was taken aback by their shift in tone. People began to filter in through the tent entrance, but Abel remained standing at the end of the row, seemingly waiting for an answer.

"Get out," Dallas hissed under his breath. "They won't know you."

"They all know me." Abel winked. "I just have one of those faces." They slid into the metal chair they had been standing beside and crossed their legs. They pulled out their gold cigarette case and the matching holder, still not taking their eyes away from Dallas as members of the congregation greeted one another and started filling the seats.

Dallas took a deep breath, dragging his nails over the pulpit's wood and digging runs into the dark-stained pine. The seats continued to fill, but he could not take his eyes off the whirlwind of gnats in the center aisle. The longer he looked, the more he wondered if the shivering blades of grass were from the wind or from maggots squirming in the gore that was embedded in the dirt.

The keyboardist took her seat and gave Dallas a questioning look before striking up a little warm-up tune. They all had the same wondering in their eyes. They wanted to know where Blue was.

In the year since the Church of New Lazarus had opened its doors, Blue had never missed a Sunday—not one. He had never been sick. And Dallas had never really thought about it until now. It had just been part of his saintly glow. God's Messenger was not supposed to wither or falter.

Maybe it was the devil in their midst. Dallas could not help but wonder if that was the cause. If simple exposure to the adversary was like breathing in black mold. If the corruption in Blue's lungs was just the devil's black claws, squeezing the pink sacs with the intention of making them rupture.

Dallas forced another breath to circulate by pulling it through his mouth and pushing it out his nose. His chest hurt. The congregation's eyes were all staring at him, shiny little wet balls without a single thought behind them.

"Good morning, church." Dallas straightened a little behind the pulpit and forced a smile. It didn't feel real on his face. He wondered if it looked real to them. "I'm sure you're wondering where Reverend Blue is this morning."

There were a few murmurs and nodding heads.

"Well, he woke up this morning feeling a bit under the weather," Dallas said. His hands were shaking and sweating. He let go of the pulpit and wiped them on the sides of his suit jacket, trying to pass it off as smoothing out his lapels. "And he wanted to be here. I had to practically tie him down to get him to stay in bed. He asked me to lead you in song and prayer so today, I ask that we all pray for his recovery." He turned his head towards the keyboardist. "Sister, if you will please lead us into 'Go Tell It on the Mountain'..."

"Come on now, Pastor Dallas," Abel's voice rose and cut off the shrill starting notes in their infancy. "It is Revival Week. Give us a proper sermon. We all believe that you can."

Dallas fought to keep his facial expressions in check, but he could feel his smile shriveling at the edges.

"Revival is about setting ourselves on fire for the Lord," Dallas shot back. "Maybe this is God's way of saying He wants the congregation to lead today."

"Pastor, with all respect," Sister Marge Elsie piped up from her back row. "We need to hear the Word today. There are many questions that the Lord has set upon my heart."

"Do you hear that?" Abel asked. "The devil is casting a long shadow, still." They grinned and set their teeth against the end of their cigarette holder. "You can do it, pastor. It isn't brain surgery, is it?"

Having his own words flung back at him made him want to spit in the devil's face, but Dallas swallowed his fury and nodded instead.

"All right," he said, then cleared his throat. "I will be happy to speak, but first, let us sing God's praise." He gestured to the keyboardist again, a bit desperately. "Sister, please, 'Go Tell It on the Mountain'."

The woman at the keyboard gave him a strange look, but she began to play again, and in staggering unison, the congregation started to sing.

CHAPTER SEVENTEEN

POWER IN THE BLOOD

After dismissing the congregation for lunch, Dallas returned home. He did not linger in the reception hall or underneath the white revival tent. He did not shake hands and smile and pray over anyone who needed a little extra care after the sermon. It was what Blue would have done, but Dallas could not tear himself away from the pulpit fast enough. Marge Elsie was the last to leave the tent, and she looked like she wanted to say something to him, but he did not stop to give her the time of day.

Dallas slammed the front door behind him and stomped into the kitchen. He went to prop his cane up between a cabinet and the refrigerator, but the rubber stopper skidded over the linoleum and the whole device went crashing to the floor. Dallas stared at it for a long minute, all the rage he had kept down since Abel had appeared that morning churned inside of his stomach. He clenched his teeth so hard that it sent a stab of pain up to his temple and he slammed his fists against the kitchen table. The wood shivered violently underneath the blows. Dallas let out a scream and hit it again, driving the sides of his fists against the center and wishing to God that he could split it in half.

"Goddammit!" he snarled, spitting flecks of blood onto the wood and smearing them out with his own pale hands. "God! Fucking! Dammit!"

"Mercy, what a mouth you have on you," Abel said. Dallas' head came up and he nearly threw up his heart.

"What are you doing here?" Dallas demanded.

"Watching you have a tantrum, at present." Abel moved from the kitchen entrance where they had been standing and walked around to stand closer to the sink. They reached down and picked up Dallas' cane, propping it up against the cabinets. This time, it stayed put.

"He is in the other room!" Dallas swept his arm across the table, pushing off the plastic napkin holder and the singular cup half-full of sweet tea that was resting on top. Both objects bounced off the floor as soon as they landed. Napkins went flying, drifting like seagulls into the waiting river of tea that was cutting a new path underneath the table. "I don't understand! Goddammit!"

"Stop swearing." Abel folded their arms across their chest. "Take a deep breath. Maybe two. What don't you understand?"

"You're supposed to be on my side!" Dallas dropped his face into his hands. They were sticky and they stung.

"Where did you get that impression?" Abel asked. "I can't help you if you're screaming."

Dallas dragged his hands down his face, digging his nails into his skin as he went. He snagged a ragged corner on his bottom lip and ripped it open. He did not care.

"That was humiliating." Dallas sniffed hard and choked. "I stumbled all the way through that sermon."

"I will say that it was not very inspiring," Abel told him. "But that comes with practice, doesn't it? There's a certain brand of showmanship that you haven't found yet. It will come."

"Showmanship." Dallas ground his teeth again. He wanted to hit something, but he was tired of striking the table. He wanted to slam his fist into his head. Maybe that would make everything better. "This isn't what I wanted."

"Things rarely end up going exactly as you think they will," Abel said. "That does not mean you are not accomplishing what you set out to do."

"I fail to see it," Dallas groaned. "I don't...!" He couldn't stop himself. He slammed his open palm against the side of his head. It felt good. The sudden, bright stripe of pain brought some clarity. He hit himself again, striking the other side. Then he used both hands at the same time, bludgeoning the sides of his head. For one dazed, glorious second, he was lost in the pain and in the buzzing noise his ears were making from the repeated blows.

"Dallas," Blue's voice was raspy like sandpaper. Feverishly warm hands grabbed Dallas by the wrists and pulled his hands away from the sides of his head. Dallas looked up, seeing double for half a second. Blue's face went from two fuzzy, indistinct shapes to one solid visage. The reverend's short blonde hair stuck up straight on one side from where he had been sleeping, and his whole face was red. He looked almost worse than when Dallas had left him.

"What are you doing?" Blue asked. He cleared his throat, sounding like he was trying to stop a cough. Dallas stared at him for another minute and then pulled away, brushing his curls away from his face.

"You're out of bed," Dallas said. He looked down at the puddle of tea he was standing in. "I'll clean this up."

"Did something happen?" Blue hocked and moved to spit into the sink. Abel stepped aside to allow it, but Blue did not seem to notice that they were there at all.

Dallas' eyes went from the reverend to the devil, who just shrugged and lit a new cigarette.

"You can't..." Dallas dragged his hand across his mouth. His torn lip left behind a rust-colored smear across his knuckles.

Blue straightened and turned back to face Dallas. His larynx bobbed as every muscle in his throat contracted and fought against the bellowing cough that attempted to squeeze out of his lungs. His hands trembled, slightly, and he gripped the counter behind him like he was afraid of falling over.

'The Voice of God,' Dallas thought. "The Voice of God is trapped in his throat.'

And the devil was right there. The devil was right there, and Blue could not see them.

Those were the same penetrating eyes that Dallas had always felt could see right through him. They looked puffy and tired. They were surrounded by crust.

'Just a man, after all. A man with a divine gift he can't even use.'

"Dallas?" Blue thumped his fist against his chest.

"Let's get you back to bed." Dallas broke out of his trance and shook his head.

"I need to take a shower," Blue said. "I am going to preach tonight."

"Tomorrow," Dallas said absentmindedly. He looped his arm through Blue's and started to walk him back towards bed. The action flashed a memory across his brain of his grandfather, right at the beginning of the end. "I preached this morning," Dallas continued. "I can do it again tonight."

"Were they receptive?" Blue sagged a bit as soon as they crossed the threshold of the bedroom.

"The Word of God is evergreen," Dallas said. "I am only the messenger. So, of course they liked it." Dallas turned Blue around so that he could sit down on the edge of the bed. The reverend closed his eyes and pushed his fingers against the bridge of his nose.

"I feel terrible," Blue admitted. Dallas nodded and stroked his hair.

"Lay down," he said. "We will be fine without you."

That evening, Dallas preached from his wheelchair. All the physical exertion from the morning's sermon had finally caught up with him. This time, the notes were mostly his own. He had only borrowed a little bit from Blue. After putting the reverend back to bed, he had cleaned up the mess in the kitchen and then spent the afternoon scribbling out a sermon of his own. It still lacked Blue's fire, he was perfectly aware of that, but he kept thinking about what Abel had said. Showmanship. It would come.

Still, he kept it short. He didn't want to lose anyone. It was easier than he figured it would be to pad out the service with hymns and testimonials. They ended it with a good old-fashioned altar call. He knew that always got people buzzing for the Lord.

It was a bizarre turn of events. Only a month before all this he would have been the one standing in front of the altar while a dozen unwanted hands pressed against him, praying for his recovery from a condition that he did not even have a name for. They prayed that the Lord would heal his back and take the pain away. They never prayed for a diagnosis. They never prayed for sound medical treatment. It was all in God's hands, and He could take it away. But He never had, even though Dallas believed that He could, if He wanted to. All this time, Dallas simply thought that he had not earned his healing. It would come at a time when God could look at him and say 'well done, my good and faithful servant'.

It seemed so long ago. A different lifetime altogether. Now they pressed their hands against each other. They prayed for Blue. They spoke in Tongues. They shouted and screamed and jumped up and down like devils dancing on a bed of coals. Not a single one of them looked upright, pure, or righteous in that moment. They looked like flustered chickens packed together in a coop.

Sister Marge Elsie was the only one who was not screaming. Usually, she led the altar calls. She was always the first to go stumbling towards the pulpit, hands raised to

Heaven while babbling in Tongues. She always wailed the loudest with tears streaming down her face until the collar of her red dress was soaked. Now, she was the only member of the congregation still seated. She remained planted in her back row, staring straight ahead.

Dallas rose from his chair. He grabbed his cane from behind the pulpit and stepped down from the makeshift platform, making his way across the grass towards the back row. He passed every thrashing, praying soul on the way. He nearly tripped over a few of them.

Finally, he reached the final row. He grabbed the back of a metal chair and sat down in front of Marge Elsie, searching her face and wishing he could read her mind.

"Is something wrong, sister?" Dallas asked. Marge Elsie finally shifted her gaze to meet his and shook her head.

"I think I was wrong about you," Marge Elsie said. "I think we all were." She looked around the tent. "I think we have made a mistake."

"A mistake?" Dallas echoed. He tightened his grip on the head of his cane.

Marge Elsie sucked in her cheeks. "I don't think God is in this place," she said. "Between you and me, I don't know why He would want to be. I think the devil has been with us a lot longer than we thought, and poor Reverend Blue—he caught it too late." Her leg started to bounce, and she adjusted her skirt nervously over her knee. "The Bible says that even Satan disguises himself as an angel of light."

"What are you saying?" Dallas asked.

"A lot of things make sense," Marge Elsie kept going. "Ever since you started on all this, changing your name and wearing boy's clothes, your poor grandfather fell sick. And we all blamed the fact that you never had a father and that your mother left early. You were a prime vessel for Satan's work, and we all failed to see it. Maybe we could have done better as your church, but I think it's too late for you. Twice today you spoke the Word of the Lord, and not once did I feel a stir. Not once. So I don't believe that God can work through you, Dallas, or Delta—whatever I am supposed to call you. I believe that you speak with Satan's forked tongue in your head. And so I will say—" she slammed her hand down on her Bible. "Get thee behind me, Satan!"

Her voice was so loud that it rose above the congregation's prayers. Dallas stood up, every thought a sudden jumble of anger and fear.

"How dare you!" he shouted back. He was not sure what was worse, the accusation itself, or the idea that others might hear her. Worse, that they might agree. He would lose control of them. All of them.

'You're going to lose them.' Abel's voice echoed in his head.

"How dare you!" she hissed back. "Liar! Impersonator! Deceiver! Devil!" Her hand thumped against her Bible with every vicious syllable. "Bless me, oh God, put this devil behind me!"

At first, Dallas did not even realize that he had struck her. The clarity came when the blood welled up from her temple and he saw her eyes flash white. He looked down and saw that he was clutching his cane like a baseball bat, and there were a few strands of matted dark hair caked in blood on the very end.

The hesitation lasted only a second. He did not stop to consider anything else before he struck again. Marge Elsie crumpled and her head bounced off the seat of a metal chair as she went down. Dallas kept swinging. It was impossible to stop. He was not sure how many times he hit her, and he did not see where every blow managed to land, but his cane kept striking something.

A few sets of hands grabbed onto his shoulders and pulled him back. Dallas snarled and wiggled free to straighten up on his own. He gripped the slick end of his cane like it was the only thing keeping him anchored to the ground.

"It is the devil's work!" Dallas cried out. He was shaking so hard he could barely stand. His knees were weak and threatened to buckle, but he remained stubbornly upright. "She had the eyes and tongue of the devil and she spoke baneful profanities in this House of the Lord." Dallas went to push his hand through his curls and paused. His fingers were covered in gore.

"Maybe you should go home, Dallas." Brother Leon set a hand against his back. "You seem mighty tired to me—"

"It is pastor," Dallas muttered. "It is Pastor Dallas, I am a pastor of this church." He cast a look around the congregation, daring any one of them to challenge him. "We cannot stop praying. There is sickness within this church, a disease unleashed by the Adversary that is eating us alive from the inside. We must return to the altar where every knee shall bow and every tongue shall confess. I am calling for more than a full Revival tonight, church!" He raised his voice. "God has shown that there is no place for false righteousness! Give yourselves over to Him, or you shall be eaten by the worms!"

Every member of the congregation fell to their knees and began to pray. The smell of blood was still sharp in the air. It covered everything else. Dallas slid his hand down the side of his cane, collecting more blood on his fingertips before raising it to the light.

He smiled. He could not help it.

"There is power," he swallowed hard. "There is power, oh, wonder-workin' power in the blood." He stuck his fingertips into his mouth and sucked Marge Elsie's blood off his skin. Her blood was hot and bitter, but he did not mind the taste.

CHAPTER EIGHTEEN

AMAZING GRACE

It was well past midnight before Dallas finally slept. When he was finally able to close his eyes, he dreamt that he was sitting on the floor of a narrow hallway across from a red door. There was barely enough room for his legs to stretch out, and even with his back against the wall, he could touch his toes against either side of the frame. He did not want to open the door, but he knew that he had to. He had to see what was on the other side. The air smelled slightly sour—like pickles. The breeze coming from underneath the door was cold, and there was a beastly sound coming from the other side. A smothered sort of grunting and groaning.

Dallas finally gathered up enough courage to stand. As soon as he touched the knob, the door slid open. The other side was a morgue—he knew that somehow, even though it did not look like one. It looked more like the inside of the church trailer, but in the place of a pulpit there was a steel table with a heavy white sheet draped over the top of what looked like a body.

Dallas moved closer to the table, even though he was afraid to lift the sheet and peer underneath it. He did not know how long the body had been there, or what it would look like, and the aisle stretched on forever. It was an agonizing walk all the way down, what he calculated inside of his dream as days.

The table shook as he approached. That ghastly, smothered sound came again as the body writhed underneath the white sheet. Dallas stopped inches away, his hand poised mid-air to grab the cloth. His breath was a caught lump in his throat. He was terrified down to the bone, but he had no choice.

For some reason, he had no choice.

If he had to do it, it was better that it was done all at once. Dallas jumped forward and grabbed the sheet, ripping it away as quickly as he could.

The corpse underneath was rotten all the way through. The skin had gone putrid green with bulging black veins making patterns along the shriveled surface. Gruesome autopsy scars, turned almost brown from exposure, roped their way down the body's chest and across its collarbone. The thickest scar running down the length of the sternum interrupted a black tattoo of a vulture, ironically contorted by death.

Dallas choked and covered his mouth, setting one of his fingers between his teeth. The dead body did not look like it could be Blue, but it was undeniably him. Dallas bent to pick up the sheet to cover the corpse back up, but it kept slipping from his fingers. He growled in frustration and kept trying, but the table shook again, and he cried out. Dallas abandoned the sheet and sprang back. Blue's body was writhing on the steel table, with his black-rimmed mouth hanging open and his blind eyes staring straight up. That gut-wrenchingly terrible sound was coming from his mouth, and Dallas could not stand it.

"No, no." Dallas climbed onto the table and pinned Blue's body underneath his. He drove his knees down onto the corpse's arms and sat on his ruined chest. "No, Blue, please. You don't speak for God anymore. You need to be quiet." There was a bottle of glue in his hand. He didn't know how it got there, but he knew what to do with it. He grabbed a pair of steel tongs from the table and stuck them down into Blue's gaping mouth. Blue's corpse growled and bit down on the cold metal. Dallas yelped again and pulled the tongs back. He slammed the butt of the handle against Blue's rotten teeth, again and again, until they cracked and the corpse's jaw slackened. Dallas pushed the tongs through the opening again and grabbed Blue's tongue. He pulled it out of the dead reverend's mouth. The repulsive gray muscle was as dry as a bone.

Dallas drizzled the glue on top of Blue's tongue and then shoved it back inside his mouth, pressing it up against the roof. The table rocked as Blue struggled, and Dallas was afraid that they would both topple, but he stayed sitting on the corpse's chest. Blue made another awful, mournful sound—and Dallas pushed his hands down over his ears.

"Why won't you stop?" Dallas choked on his own anger. "Why won't you stop?" He poured more glue into the crevice that separated Blue's lips and then pushed them together. The corpse jerked and groaned, and the steel table rocked violently.

Dallas leaned over and grabbed onto Blue's shoulders. The table rocked again, tipping over onto two legs, and they both went toppling. The fall lasted forever, but Dallas' head hit the ground, and the pain that burst across his skull was enough to wake him up.

His nose hurt and all he could taste was blood. Dallas reached up and touched the bridge tenderly, feeling for a break. It was swollen, for sure, but probably not broken. He shoved his hand underneath his nose to catch the blood that was flowing freely from his nostrils.

There was something stuck to his palm. Dallas licked the salty blood away from his lips as he took a closer look. It was a little crinkled yellow tube with a red spout and 'CRAZY GLUE' written in bold blue letters on the side.

Dallas peeled the tube up from his skin and winced because it stung. There was a hard patch of glue left behind in the center of his palm, but he knew it would not come up with a simple peel.

That low, ugly sound from his dream came again. Dallas' stomach clenched and he looked over, taking stock of where he was. He was home. He did not remember walking through the doors. He did not remember getting undressed and crawling into bed. He did not even remember falling asleep. Yet, he was beside his bed, and Blue was there too— hanging halfway off the side. The rough, hacking gargle was coming from the blond reverend, whose bloody lips were stuck together with a bright and shiny seal. He could not cough, so everything was being expelled from his nose. He was covered down to his chin in slime and struggling to breathe.

Dallas swallowed his horror and crawled towards him. He tried to take Blue's head in his hands, but the reverend warned him with a growl. Blue slid off the bed entirely and landed against the floor. He grabbed Dallas' curls and wrenched his head around like he was trying to slam it into whatever he could reach—the bedside table, a wall—anything. Dallas pulled himself free. Blue might have been angry, but he was still weak. The sickness still ravaged his body. Dallas crawled backwards, searching blindly for anything he could grab hold of to defend himself. Blue tore at his own mouth, doing nothing to remove the glue and only pulling up chunks of his own flesh.

Dallas' back hit the wall and he sat there for a moment. His chest heaved as he tried to catch his breath and he watched Blue to see what he would do next. The reverend's shoulders sagged as he huffed. He expelled another cough through his nose and a miserable breath rattled in his chest. His head drooped, and he clawed at his mouth again. It was useless. Dallas knew it was useless.

But he had done it in his sleep. There was still blood on his hands, and not all of it was his own. Some of it was dried-up and brown.

He was starting to feel light-headed. He bunched up the hem of his shirt and stuffed it into his nostrils to try and stop the blood flow.

Had he really killed Marge Elsie? Or had that all been a dream, too? The lines between what was real and what was not were so blurred. The last thing he remembered with any clarity was Abel, standing by his kitchen sink and lighting a brand-new cigarette.

Dallas closed his eyes and leaned his head against the wall. Even with his eyes shut, the world was still spinning. His limbs were cold and heavy with pins and needles in his fingertips. The world behind his lids was all fireworks.

He worried about passing out. He had no idea what Blue might do to him while he slept. Then again, he welcomed it. Then he wouldn't have to listen to that awful, disgusting, snotty hacking.

The fireworks died out. The world went quiet. If he didn't wake up again, he didn't care.

Sunlight was a knife across his vision. Dallas groaned and raised a hand to try and cover his eyes. His neck was stiff. His back was stiffer. There had been no dreams after the nightmare with Blue, but now his mouth was dry and his tongue felt gummy, and everything tasted like rust.

Blue was gone. That much he could see. Panic gripped him for a moment and Dallas braced himself to stand while every muscle screamed in protest.

"Good morning," Abel's familiar voice drifted over. "Rise and shine."

"I feel like Hell," Dallas said.

"You look worse than that," Abel moved to stand in front of him and crouched. "I am going to help you up. Ready?

Here we go." They slid their arms underneath Dallas'. "Lean on me for support. On my count—"

"Where is Blue?" Dallas interrupted them.

"One, two—three." Abel pulled him to his feet. "You have a sermon to give this morning."

"Do I?" Dallas rubbed the back of his head and sniffed. The caked blood around his nostrils was itchy and unpleasant to breathe through. "I thought I had lost them. Last night, I—"

"Let me tell you one thing about people," Abel said. "Especially these Parable-of-the-Sower types. They are like clay. They're formless. They need to be manipulated or they don't serve any purpose. And you were close. You almost lost them. That bit where you bludgeoned that biddy to death—well, it was fun, but it wasn't clever. Exhausting them with fervent prayer, that was a step in the right direction—but a few still went home and turned over a thought or two. However, they are afraid, now, and you can use that. Fear is a beginner's weapon, almost anyone can pick it up to wield. I believe that you can."

"Thanks," Dallas said dryly. His head hurt so badly that all he wanted to do was lay back down. "You didn't answer my question, though. Where is Blue?"

"Come and see," Abel said. "I will show you. But first we have to rinse you off."

Dallas obliged. He allowed Abel to help him over to the shower and rinse him off. The cold water circled the drain in dark orange streaks while Dallas blew the crust from his nose and soaped the clumps out of his curls. When he stepped out, he sat his aching body down on the toilet while the devil helped him dress. It was not dignified, but there was not a single part of him that did not hurt. Even after the simple labor of a shower, he was breathing heavily.

Abel dressed him in a suit that he did not recognize. It was deep, sophisticated red with a crisp white button-down underneath. The bolo tie that the devil slid up towards his throat was one of Blue's—a detailed gold bird.

"Where-?" Dallas started to ask.

"The suit? I thought you might like it," Abel said. "And you needed something new." They knelt to slip Dallas' shoes onto his feet and then helped him up. "I cleaned up your wheelchair," they said. "You let it get gross. There was blood all over the rims and on the seat. Don't do that again, alright?"

"Alright." It did not feel real. None of this felt right. The devil walked by his side and led Dallas out towards the living room. The front door was open and his yellow-and-chrome wheelchair was waiting on the porch, brighter than a throne.

Dallas took his seat and allowed himself to settle in. His back felt bruised and it probably was, but fully cleansed and newly clothed, he felt better than he had in days.

"Are you ready?" Abel asked.

"Yes." Dallas nodded. "Let's go."

"Hold on," Abel held up a finger. "One more thing." They disappeared into the house and reappeared seconds later with Blue's wide-brimmed black hat in their hands. They set it down on top of Dallas' red curls and then took a step back, scanning their brown eyes up and down his form before nodding their approval.

"Very handsome," Abel said. "Now you look the part, Pastor Dallas."

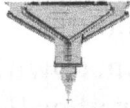

everend Blessing Easton was found dead swinging from the branch of a champion oak tree that stood proudly beside the white church trailer. The rope around his neck was the same braided silver polyethylene that they had used to erect the revival tent, and it cut a nasty red ligature mark into his neck. He had taken enough time to put on something other than his bedclothes. He was wearing a bright red dress shirt, although the collar was open and the small gold cross necklace he always wore. His jeweled cross earring dangled heavily from his lobe, and his gold Rolex watch flashed from his mottled, limp wrist. There were rings on every one of his bloated, grey fingers. His face was a ghoulish shade of purple, and his cornflower blue eyes bugged out from their sockets. His beautifully shaped mouth was crusted in blood and glue and had turned almost black from the lack of oxygen. There was more snot on his face and neck than Dallas remembered, probably from all the breathing he had been trying to do. It covered his mouth and chin, thick and wet like an amniotic sac.

The congregation was gathered underneath him, muttering quietly amongst themselves—but they fell silent and parted like the Red Sea when they saw Dallas coming. Dallas could no longer feel the devil behind him, but he knew that they were still there. All this time since the crossroads, they had never left.

Dallas stopped just shy of placing himself underneath Blue's swinging corpse. It was a strange sight to see him so high up near the clouds—the ascending Christ figure. Dallas scrunched up his mouth.

"Why has no one cut him down?" he asked.

"We were waiting..." Brother Hugh started to speak, but his words died on his tongue. They were all staring at Dallas—watching, waiting. They all seemed to be, collectively, holding their breath.

Now, Dallas understood what the devil had meant. He raised his chin and held up his hands at the same time with his palms pointed upwards to the sky.

"The greatest tragedy here lies in our number having been deceived for so long," Dallas said, fighting to keep his voice level. "But God has purged the sickness from our midst. And now, we will pray." He tilted his head back. A beam of sunlight penetrated the swaying canopy of oak leaves and landed on his face. He closed his eyes and soaked it up. "If you cannot find words, then you need only to sing the chorus of 'Amazing Grace'. For we have been led out of the Valley of the Shadow of Death and now we praise God, praise God, praise God—" It was the first time Dallas had really allowed himself to sing, and the first time he didn't mind his soft, clear voice being heard above all others. The congregation brought themselves in closer to one another, joining hands and raising their voices in the old hymn's chorus.

A cool breeze, a taste of Autumn teasing the change of seasons, brushed against Dallas' cheek. The air smelled like overripe peaches and like Blue's Aqua Velva cologne.

And underneath it all, a thin ribbon of tobacco smoke. A sweet reminder of his benison.

It completely covered the stench of rot.

About the Author

Sirius is a lover of glory, gore, and monsters. They are a queer, nonbinary artist living in the hot and bothered South; currently residing in a little spot that has been dubbed 'Halloweentown', North Carolina. They are the writer of The Draonir Saga, the Dread South Series, and the Gentleman Demon Series.

Sirius began writing at a young age and started exploring the publishing industry when they were thirteen. With many bumps along the way, they have learned a lot and grown in the craft that they would consider their one true love. Queer characters, gothic aesthetics, and royal drama (fantasy of manners) form the foundation of their storytelling.

When they are not writing, they work as a professional drag performer, weaving the characters from their stories into visual art for the stage.

9 798218 417604